"Come, Zoe, it's time to prepare you for your wedding night."

It suddenly sank into her. She belonged to the Sheikh. A man they called The Beast. She was married to him. *Married.*

Zoe didn't resist as the women settled her in the center of the bed. She knelt on the mattress, her hands folded in front of her, her head bent down.

She was taking a leap of faith, believing she could use this marriage to her advantage, when she might have given up more than her freedom to a man who was a dangerous stranger.

What had she done?

Pure terror clamped her chest. She felt the room closing in on her as she tried to gulp in the hot air. She blinked as dark spots danced before her eyes and she remembered her cousin's words.

"If you aren't to Nadir's liking, he can throw you back."

Susanna Carr has been an avid romance reader since she read her first at the age of ten. Although romance novels were not allowed in her home, she always managed to sneak one in from the local library, or from her twin sister's secret stash.

After attending college and receiving a degree in English Literature, Susanna pursued a romance-writing career. She has written sexy contemporary romances for several publishers, and her work has been honoured with awards for contemporary and sensual romance.

Susanna lives in the Pacific Northwest with her family. When she isn't writing, she enjoys reading romance and connecting with readers online. Visit her website at www.susannacarr.com

This is Susanna's sizzling sexy debut for Mills & Boon® Modern™ Romance!

THE TARNISHED JEWEL OF JAZAAR

BY
SUSANNA CARR

First published in Great Britain 2012
by Mills & Boon, an imprint of Harlequin (UK) Limited.
Harlequin (UK) Limited, Eton House, 18-24 Paradise Road,
Richmond, Surrey TW9 1SR

© Susanna Carr 2012

ISBN: 978 0 263 89093 8

Harlequin (UK) policy is to use papers that are natural, renewable and recyclable products and made from wood grown in sustainable for- ests. The logging and manufacturing process conform to the legal environmental regulations of the country of origin.

Printed and bound in Spain
by Blackprint CPI, Barcelona

THE TARNISHED JEWEL OF JAZAAR

To Lucy Gilmour, for her insights and encouragement.
Thanks for making my dream come true!

CHAPTER ONE

DARKNESS descended on the desert as the black SUV came to a halt in front of the village's inn, a large but plain building. The arches and columns that guarded the courtyard were decorated with flower garlands. Strands of lights were wrapped around thick palm trees. Sheikh Nadir ibn Shihab heard the native music beyond the columns. In the distance, fireworks shot off and sprayed into the night sky, announcing his arrival.

It was time to meet his bride.

Nadir felt no excitement. There was no curiosity and no dread. Having a wife was a means to an end. It was not an emotional choice but a civilized arrangement. An arrangement he was making because of one rash, emotional reaction two years ago.

He pushed his thoughts aside. He wasn't going to think about the injustice now. With this marriage he would repair his reputation and no one would question his commitment to the traditional way of life in the kingdom of Jazaar.

Nadir stepped out of the car and his *dishdasha* was plastered against his muscular body as his black cloak whipped in the strong wind. The white headdress billowed behind him. Nadir found the traditional clothes confining, but today he wore them out of respect to custom.

He saw his younger brother approach. Nadir smiled at

the unusual sight of Rashid wearing traditional garb. They greeted each other with an embrace.

"You are very late for your wedding," Rashid said in a low and confidential tone.

"It doesn't start until I arrive," Nadir replied as he pulled back.

Rashid shook his head at his brother's arrogance. "I mean it, Nadir. This is not the way to make amends with the tribe."

"I'm aware of it. I got here as quickly as I could." He had spent most of his wedding day negotiating with two warring tribes over a sacred spot of land. It was more important than a wedding feast. Even if it was his own wedding.

"That's not good enough for the elders," Rashid said as they walked toward the hotel. "In their eyes you showed them the ultimate disrespect two years ago. They won't forgive your tardiness."

Nadir was not in the mood to be lectured by his younger brother. "I'm marrying the woman of their choice, aren't I?"

The marriage was a political alliance with an influential tribe who both respected and feared him. Nadir had heard that his nickname in this part of the desert was The Beast. And, like mere mortals who knew they had angered a demon god, the elders were willing to sacrifice a young virgin as his bride.

Nadir approached the row of elders, who were dressed in their finest. Glimpsing the solemn faces of the older men, Nadir knew Rashid was right. They were not happy with him. If this tribe wasn't so important for his plans to modernize the country, Nadir would ignore their existence.

"My humblest apologies." Nadir greeted the elders, bowing low and offering his deepest regrets for his tardiness. He didn't care if these men felt slighted by his delay, but he went through the motions.

He had no use for the prolonged greeting ritual, but he had to be diplomatic. He was already battling political retribution from the elders, and had countered it by showing a willingness to marry a woman from their tribe. That maneuver should have improved relations with the tribal leaders, but Nadir sensed they were anything but honored.

The elders politely ushered him into the courtyard as the ancient chant accompanied by drums pulsed in the air. It tugged at something deep in Nadir, but he wasn't going to join in. While the guests were happy that the Sheikh was marrying one of their own, he wasn't pleased about the turn of events.

"Do you know anything about the bride?" Rashid whispered into Nadir's ear. "What if she's unsuitable?"

"It's not important," Nadir quietly informed his brother. "I have no plans to live as husband and wife. I will marry her and take her to bed, but once the wedding ceremonies are over she will live in the harem at the Sultan's palace. She will have everything she needs and I'll have my freedom. If all goes well we will never set eyes on each other again."

Nadir surveyed the crowd. Men were on one side of the aisle, dressed in white, chanting and clapping as they provoked the women on the other side to dance faster. The women's side was a riot of color liberally streaked with gold. The women silently taunted the men, their hips undulating to the edge of propriety. Their loose-fitting garments stretched and strained over voluptuous curves.

His presence was suddenly felt. He felt the ripple of awareness through the crowd. The music ended abruptly as everyone froze, staring at him. He felt like an unwelcome guest at his own wedding.

Nadir was used to seeing wariness in the eyes of everyone from statesmen to servants. International businesses accused him of being as devious as a jackal when he thwarted their attempts to steal Jazaar's resources. Journalists declared that he enforced the Sultan's law with the ruthless sting of a scorpion's tail. He had even been compared to a viper when he'd protected Jazaar with unwavering aggression from bloodthirsty rebels. His countrymen might be afraid to look him in the eye, but they knew he would take care of them by any means necessary.

Nadir strode down the aisle with Rashid one step behind him. The guests slowly regained their festive spirits, singing loudly as they showered him with rose petals. They seemed indecently relieved that his three-day marriage ceremony had commenced. He frowned at the men's wide smiles and the women's high-pitched trills. It was as if they believed they had appeased The Beast's hunger.

He kept his gaze straight ahead on the end of the courtyard. A dais sat in the center. A couple of divans flanked two golden throne-like chairs. His bride sat in one, waiting for him with her head tucked low and her hands in her lap.

Nadir slowed down when he saw that his bride wore an ethnic wedding dress in deep crimson. A heavy veil concealed her hair and framed her face before cascading down her shoulders and arms. Her fitted bodice was encrusted with gold beads, hinting at the small breasts and slender waist underneath. Her delicate hands, decorated with an ornate henna design, lay against the voluminous brocade skirt.

He frowned as he studied the woman. There was something different, something *wrong* about the bride. He halted in the middle of the aisle as the realization hit him like a clap of thunder.

"Nadir!" Rashid whispered harshly.

"I see." His tone was low and fierce as the shock reverberated inside him.

The woman before him was no Jazaari bride, fit for a sheikh.

She was an outcast. A woman no man would marry.

The tribal leaders had tricked him. Nadir stood very still as his anger flared. He had agreed to marry a woman of the tribe's choosing in a gesture of good faith. In return they had given him the American orphaned niece of one of their families.

It was an insult, he thought grimly as he ruthlessly reined in his emotions. It was also a message. The tribe thought that Nadir was too Western and modern to appreciate a traditional Jazaari bride.

"How dare they?" Rashid said in growl. "We're leaving now. Once the Sultan hears about this we will formally shun this tribe and—"

"No." Nadir's decision was swift and certain. He didn't like it, but all his instincts told him it was for the greater good. "I accepted their choice."

"Nadir, you don't have to."

"Yes, I do."

The tribe expected him to refuse this woman as his bride. They wanted him to defy tradition and prove that he didn't appreciate the Jazaari way of life.

He couldn't do that. Not again.

And the elders knew it.

Nadir's eyes narrowed into slits. He would accept this unworthy woman as his bride. And once the wedding was over he would destroy the elders in this tribe one by one.

"I must protest," Rashid said. "A sheikh does not marry an outcast."

"I agree, but I need a bride, and any woman from this

tribe will do. One woman is just as much trouble as the next."

"But…"

"Don't worry, Rashid. I am changing my plans. I won't let her live in the Sultan's palace. I will send her into seclusion at the palace in the mountains." He would hide this woman—and any evidence that he had been shamed by this tribe. No one would ever know how he had paid a huge dowry for such an inferior bride.

Nadir forced his feet to move, his white-hot anger turning to ice as he approached his bride. He noticed that the woman's face was pale against her dark red lips and kohled eyes. A thick rope of rubies and diamonds edged along her hairline. She had a tangle of necklaces around her throat and a long column of gold bangles on both arms.

She was dressed like a Jazaari bride, but it was obvious that she wasn't the real thing. Her downcast eyes and prim posture couldn't hide her bold nature. There was a defiant tilt to her head and a brash energy about her.

The woman also had an earthy sexiness, he decided. A proper bride would be shy and modest. She looked like a mysterious and exotic maiden who should be dancing barefoot by a bonfire on a dark desert night.

His bride cautiously glanced from beneath her lashes and he captured her startled gaze. Nadir felt the impact as their eyes clashed and held.

Zoe Martin's blood raced painfully through her veins as she stared into dark, hypnotic eyes. As much as she wanted to, she couldn't look away. The eyes darkened. She felt as if she was caught in a swirling storm.

Please don't let this be the man I am marrying! She needed to trick and manipulate her husband throughout their honeymoon, but she could tell immediately this man was too dangerous for her plans.

Sheikh Nadir ibn Shihab wasn't handsome. His features were too hard, too primitive. His face was all lines and angles, from his Bedouin nose to the forceful thrust of his jaw. His cheekbones slashed down his face and a cleft scored his chin. There was a hint of softness in his full lips, but the cynical curl at the edge of his mouth warned of his impatience. She had no doubt that everyone kept a distance from him or suffered the brunt of his venomous barbs.

The pearl-white of the Sheikh's *dishdasha* contrasted with his golden-brown skin and it couldn't conceal his long, tapered body. Every move he made drew her attention to his lean and compact muscles. Zoe decided that his elegant appearance was deceiving. She had no doubt that he had been brought up in a world of wealth and privilege, but this man belonged to the harsh and unforgiving desert. He had the desert's stark beauty and its cruelty.

The Sheikh showed no expression, no emotion, but she felt a biting hot energy slamming against her. Zoe flinched, her skin stinging from his bold gaze. She wanted to rub her arms and wrap them protectively around her. She felt the inexplicable need to slough off his claim.

Claim? A flash of fear gripped Zoe as her chest tightened. Why did it feel like that? The Sheikh hadn't touched her yet.

She had the sudden overwhelming need to turn and run as fast as she could to escape. Her heart pounded in her ears, her breath rasped in her constricted throat, and although every self-preservation instinct told her to flee, she couldn't move.

"As-Salamu Alaykum," Nadir greeted as he sat down next to her.

Zoe shivered at the rough, masculine sound. His voice was soft, but the commanding tone coiled around her body, tugging at something dark and unknown inside her. The muscles low in her abdomen tingled with awareness.

"It's a pleasure to meet you," he said with cool politeness.

Zoe gave a start, her excess of gold jewelry chiming from her sudden move. He'd spoken to her in English. It had been so long since she'd heard her mother tongue. Unshed tears suddenly stung her eyes and she struggled to regain her composure.

She shouldn't have been surprised that the Sheikh spoke English. He'd been educated in the United States, traveled frequently, and knew several languages as well as all the dialects spoken in Jazaar. His need to travel internationally was one of the reasons why she had agreed to marry him.

But curiosity got the better of her. She couldn't imagine this man doing something thoughtful without getting something in return. Her voice wavered as she asked, "Why are you speaking to me in English?"

"You are American. It's your language."

She gave a curt nod and kept her head down, her gaze focused on her clenched hands. It had been her language once. Until her uncle had forbidden it. "It isn't spoken here," she whispered.

"That's why I'm using it," Nadir said in an uninterested tone as he surveyed the courtyard. "English will be just our language and no one will know what we're saying."

Ah, now she understood. He wanted to create an immediate bond between them. Or at least the illusion of one. It was a clever strategy, but she wasn't going to fall for it.

"I'm not supposed to talk during the ceremony," she reminded him.

She sensed his attention back on her. The energy crackling between them grew sharper. "But I want you to talk."

Right. Was this some sort of test to see if she was a good

Jazaari bride? "My aunts gave me strict orders to keep my head down and my mouth shut."

"Whose opinions are more important to you?" She heard the arrogance in his voice. "Your aunts' or your husband's?"

Neither, she wanted to say. It was tempting, but she knew she had to play the game. "I will do as you wish." She nearly choked on the words.

His chuckle was rough and masculine. "Keep saying that and we'll get along just fine."

Zoe clenched her teeth, preventing herself from giving a sharp reply. She swallowed her retort just in time as the first elder came onto the dais. As she'd expected, the older man ignored her and spoke only to the Sheikh.

She stared at her hands in her lap and slowly squeezed her fingers together. The bite of pain didn't distract her from her troubled thoughts. She was never going to pull off the demure look. It was just a matter of time before she messed up. Her family knew it, too. The disapproving glares from her aunts were hot enough to burn a sizzling hole in her veil.

Zoe knew her appearance and manners didn't meet family expectations. They never had. Her face was much too pale and she lacked refinement and feminine charm. It didn't matter if the veil concealed her features, or if her bent head hid her big, bold eyes. They knew she wasn't a proper young woman. She talked louder than a whisper, walked faster than she should, and no matter how often she was told she never knew her place.

She was too American. Too much trouble. Simply too much.

Her relatives thought she should be timid and subservient, and they had tried to transform her using every barbaric punishment they knew. Starvation. Sleep deprivation.

Beatings. Nothing had worked. It had only made Zoe more rebellious and determined to get out of this hell. If only she had a better escape plan. If only her freedom didn't rely on pretending to be the perfect woman.

As the last elder left the dais, Zoe felt the Sheikh's intent gaze on her. She tensed but kept her focus on her hands. Did he find her lacking or did she pass inspection?

"What is your name?" the Sheikh asked her.

Zoe's eyes widened. *Seriously?* This was not something a woman wanted to hear from her husband on her wedding day. Zoe held back the urge to give him a false name. *A stripper name,* she thought with a sly smile. If only she could. But it wouldn't be worth the punishment.

"Zoe Martin," she answered.

"And how old are you?"

Old enough. She bit the tip of her tongue before she blurted out that reply. "I'm twenty-one years old."

How was it possible the Sheikh didn't know anything about her? Wasn't he curious about the woman he married? Didn't he care?

"Do I detect a Texan accent?" he asked.

Zoe bit her bottom lip as a memory of her home in Texas bloomed. The last time she had felt as if she belonged to a family. Once she had been loved and protected; now she was chattel for her uncle.

"You have a very good ear," she answered huskily. "I thought I had lost the twang." *Along with everything else.*

"Texas is a long way from here."

No kidding. But she knew what he was really asking. How the hell had she wound up in Jazaar? She'd wondered that many times herself. "My father was a doctor for a humanitarian medical organization and he met my mother when he visited Jazaar. Didn't anyone tell you about me?"

"I was told everything I needed to know."

That made her curious. What had been said about her? She wasn't sure if she wanted to know. "Such as?" she asked as she watched the servants bringing plates of food to the dais.

He shrugged. "You are part of this tribe and you are of marriageable age."

She waited a beat. "Anything else?"

"What else do I need to know?"

Her eyes widened. His indifference took her breath away, but she knew she should be grateful for it. It was better that he had not asked any questions or dug for information. He would have discovered what kind of woman he was marrying.

Zoe barely ate anything from the wedding feast. She usually had a healthy appetite—some felt too robust—but tonight the aromas and spices were overwhelming. Immediately after the meal a procession of guests approached the dais to congratulate the happy couple. She was glad that no one expected her to speak. She barely listened to what was said, too aware of the man sitting next to her.

"You will have your hands full with this one, Your Highness. She's nothing but trouble."

Zoe glanced up when she heard those words. She knew she should keep her head down, but she was surprised that someone would warn the Sheikh. Weren't they trying to get rid of her by marrying her off?

Yet she had never got along with the wife of the wealthy storekeeper. The older woman had forbidden Zoe from entering the store. But Zoe was used to being excluded and had frequently managed to make her purchases through strategy and stealth.

"She's an incredibly slow learner," the older woman continued. "It doesn't matter how hard her uncle slaps her, Zoe keeps talking back."

"Is that so?" the Sheikh drawled. "Perhaps her uncle is the slow learner and should try a new approach?"

Zoe jerked in surprise and immediately ducked her head so no one could see her expression. Was he questioning Uncle Tareef's methods? She thought men sided with one another.

"Nothing works with Zoe," the storekeeper's wife informed the Sheikh. "Once she burned the dinner. Of course she was punished. You'd think she'd learn her lesson, but the next day she poured an entire pot of hot pepper in the dinner. Her uncle had blisters inside his mouth for weeks."

"It wasn't my fault he kept trying to eat it," Zoe said as she glared at the woman. "And at least it wasn't burnt."

Zoe cringed inwardly when she recognized her mistake and immediately bent her head as if nothing happened. There was a long, silent pause and Zoe felt the Sheikh's gaze on her. She instinctively hunched her shoulders, as if that would make her smaller. Invisible.

"I hope your cooking has improved," he said.

Zoe nodded cautiously. It was a lie, but he would never find out. She was grateful that he'd ignored her outburst, surprised that he didn't comment on it.

He was probably saving it all up for later, she decided, as the tension vibrated inside her. She was going to face one monstrous lecture after the ceremony.

"When all else failed," the older woman valiantly continued, "Zoe was forced to treat the sick until she learned how to behave. She has taken care of the poor women for *years*."

Zoe knew that the task of treating the ill was reserved for servants in the tribe, but she didn't care. It was what she wanted to do. The science of nursing and the art of folk remedies fascinated her.

"Zoe," Nadir said, "you no longer have to treat the sick."

Zoe frowned, not sure how to answer. "That's not necessary. I'm not afraid of hard work and I'm very good at it."

"Zoe!" the storekeeper's wife said in a scandalized tone, her eyes dancing with delight. "A Jazaari woman must be humble."

Nadir rose from his seat and Zoe couldn't help noticing how tall and commanding he was. He motioned for the most exalted elder to approach the dais. Zoe's stomach twisted sharply and she tasted hot, bitter fear in her mouth. What was the Sheikh doing? She had displeased him. Somehow she would be punished for it.

The older woman smiled victoriously and walked away with a spring in her step as the elder approached. Zoe was angry at herself for letting the old bat rile her.

The Sheikh placed his palm against his heart and told the chief elder, "You have honored me with Zoe as my bride."

The elder couldn't hide his surprise and the nearby guests started to whisper excitedly behind their hands and veils. Zoe didn't feel any relief. Instead, she battled the trickle of suspicion. Honored? He didn't know the first thing about her.

"I gladly accept the duty to protect her and provide for her," the Sheikh continued, his voice strong and clear. "She will want for nothing."

Her suspicions deepened as the buzz of conversation swelled. What was this man up to? She had learned firsthand that when a man made those kinds of promises it was very likely he would do the opposite. Like when Uncle Tareef had promised to take her in and look after her. Instead he'd stolen her inheritance and she'd become an unpaid servant in his household.

"And as your Sheikha," Nadir announced, "she will spend her days and nights tending to me."

Zoe lowered her head as the guests cheered. Anger swirled inside her chest. The tribe was thrilled that she pleased the Sheikh. He wasn't going to let her leave his side and she wouldn't have time to nurse the sick because she had the honor of being at his beck and call.

The man had no idea how important it was for her to work. Before her parents died Zoe had volunteered at the local hospital with her mother. It had been exciting and she'd known then she wanted to have a medical career like her father's.

Her dreams of practicing medicine with her father had been shattered when her parents died in a car accident and suddenly she had found herself living in a foreign place with people she didn't know. She had suffered through the language barrier, strange food and an unwelcoming tribe. But when she'd watched the healer treat the sick, Zoe had felt she was back in familiar territory.

In a matter of months she had become the healer's assistant. It was supposed to be a punishment, but she had wanted to learn. When Zoe noticed that the poor women were reluctant to seek medical help from a male healer, she gradually took on the female patients. It was her way of continuing her family's legacy, and practicing medicine had become her lifeline.

She had finally found a way to stay away from Uncle Tareef's house and focus on something other than her difficult situation. And when she handled a medical emergency she felt the same excitement she had when she'd been back home in the local hospital. Taking care of women in need had let her find a sense of purpose. It was the one thing that kept her going.

And now the Sheikh wanted to take that away from her? Zoe closed her eyes and tried desperately to control her temper. She had to give up the one thing that interested her, the one thing she was good at, because Nadir didn't like it? It wasn't fair. She wanted to argue right here and now.

What was she upset about? Zoe slowly opened her eyes. What Nadir wanted didn't affect her life. She wasn't going to stay married long enough for him to take her interests away from her.

"I must say you surprised me."

Zoe looked at the tall and slender woman who was now sitting next to her—her cousin Fatimah. Zoe clenched her teeth as she braced herself for what she was sure would be a few unpleasant moments.

Fatimah wore a shimmering green gown. Heavy gold jewelry dripped from her ears, throat and wrists. She always made a glamorous and dramatic impact wherever she went.

"I didn't think you would do it," Fatimah told Zoe in a breezy, chatty tone. "I know how you Americans believe in love matches."

Zoe didn't respond. She had never liked her cousin, and they weren't friends. Fatimah would not form an alliance with an outcast like Zoe. Instead, she preferred to feel powerful by preying on the defenseless, and Zoe had seen her in all her destructive glory. Now she noted the dark look in her cousin's eyes. Fatimah was on the prowl for trouble and had found her target.

Her cousin bestowed a tight smile upon her. "I can't wait to tell Musad."

Zoe did her best not to flinch. "Please do."

She hoped she was getting better at not reacting to his name. Musad had once represented a fragile yet blossoming love in a world of quicksand filled with hate and indifference. Now his name reminded her that no man could be trusted.

"What should I tell our old friend?" Fatimah asked

as she studied Zoe's face closely. "Shall I send him your love?"

Zoe shrugged, refusing to let the word "love" pierce her wrung-out heart. Musad had ceased to matter a year ago, when he'd moved to America without a backward glance. She had filed him under "lesson learned."

Zoe leaned back in her chair as if she didn't have a care in the world. "Tell him what you want."

Fatimah rested her hand on Zoe's arm and leaned forward to whisper, "How can you say that, considering how *close* you were?"

Zoe felt the blood leaving her face as icy fear seeped in her veins. Fatimah knew. She saw it in the malicious glow of the woman's eyes. Somehow Fatimah knew about her forbidden liaison with Musad. She was the one who'd started the rumors that were beginning to percolate in village gossip.

Zoe had to get away. She had to silence Fatimah. If she breathed a word of this to her family…to the Sheikh…

"Zoe?"

Zoe looked up to see her aunts and other female cousins. They were smiling. Real smiles. It was unlikely that they had heard Fatimah's accusation. Zoe wanted to sag with relief.

"Come, Zoe." One of her cousins unceremoniously pulled her from her chair and her female relatives surrounded her. "It's time to prepare you for your wedding night."

Her wedding night. Her stomach twisted sharply and she battled back nausea. Her aunts smiled and giggled as they swept her out of the courtyard and up to the honeymoon suite. She hunched her shoulders as corroding fear, thick and searing hot, bled through her body. It pooled under her skin, pressing harder and harder, threatening to burst through.

It suddenly sank into her. She belonged to the Sheikh. A man they called The Beast. She was married to him. *Married.*

Her married cousins were offering words of advice, telling her how to please her husband, but Zoe didn't hear a word of it. There was a desperate energy among the women. Their laughter was a little shrill, their advice raw and uncoated.

Zoe didn't resist as the women settled her in the center of the bed. She knelt on the mattress, her hands folded in front of her, her head bent down. She wanted to jump out of bed and run, but she knew these women would bring her back and guard the bedroom.

She closed her eyes and took a deep, jagged breath. She heard the women leaving the room, their laughter harsh as they tossed her more marital advice. She had always thought her wedding day would be different. In her daydreams it had been full of laughter and joy, not to mention love.

The reality was much bleaker. Zoe slowly opened her eyes. She was marrying because she was out of options and running out of luck. She was taking a leap of faith, believing she could use this marriage to her advantage. But she might have given up more than her freedom to a man who was a dangerous stranger.

What had she done?

Pure terror clamped her chest. She felt the room closing in on her as she tried to gulp in the hot air. Dark spots danced before her eyes.

"I can't do this. I can't sleep with him," Zoe said aloud. She thought she was alone until Fatimah answered.

"He's required to consummate the marriage," her cousin

said as she straightened Zoe's skirt, making it a smooth circle on the bed. "Otherwise it's not acknowledged."

"Required?" Zoe's stomach gave a sickening twist. That sounded so clinical. So unromantic.

Fatimah cast an annoyed look in her direction. "That's why you have the last ceremony on the third day. It's based on an ancient law to celebrate the consummation of the marriage."

Zoe's jaw dropped. "Are you kidding me?"

"And if you aren't to his liking," Fatimah said, giving her a sidelong look, "he can throw you back."

Zoe frowned. "Throw me back? You mean back to your family? No, he can't. Nice try, Fatimah, but I'm not falling for another one of your lies."

"I'm not lying," Fatimah swore, flattening her hand against her chest. "The Sheikh did that to his first wife."

First wife? Zoe drew back her head and stared at her cousin as surprise tingled down her spine. What first wife? "What are you talking about?"

"Didn't anyone tell you?" Fatimah's face brightened when she realized she would get to reveal all. "Two years ago the Sheikh was married to the daughter of one of the finest families in the tribe. Yusra. You remember her?"

"Barely." Yusra had been drop-dead gorgeous, ultra feminine and the perfect Jazaari girl. Zoe had privately thought Yusra was a spoiled brat and a bit of snob. She had been glad when her family left the village.

"It was a fabulous ceremony. Unlike any I've ever seen. Don't you remember it? It was better than yours."

"I probably wasn't invited." She was an outcast. She was either ignored or bullied. Any member of the tribe could publicly humiliate her without consequence. They all knew her uncle wouldn't protect her. They had all witnessed the treatment she'd received under his cruel hand and followed his lead.

"Well, the third day of the ceremony had barely started when he tossed Yusra back to her parents." Fatimah gave a flick of her wrist, the jangle of gold bracelets loud to Zoe's ears. "In front of the entire tribe. He said she was not to his liking."

If he'd had a problem with his first choice of a wife, he was definitely not going to be pleased with her. "He had sex with her and then dumped her? Can he do that?"

"It caused a huge scandal. How is it you don't know any of this? You were living here when it happened."

Zoe probably had heard about it but thought it one of those "bonfire stories." She had heard plenty of folk tales that were designed to scare boys and girls into behaving properly.

She was in so much trouble. Her knees wobbled as a wave of fear crashed over her. If she didn't have sex with the Sheikh he would send her back to her family. If she did have sex with him she might well have had the same problem. "So basically this ancient law is a return policy?"

"It's rarely used. A man has to have a very good reason to invoke it. Unless you're a sheikh, of course. Then no one will question your actions."

"But—"

One of Zoe's aunts peeked inside the room. "Fatimah, what are you still doing here?" the woman said in a fierce whisper. "The Sheikh is coming."

"Good luck, Zoe," Fatimah said with a sly smile as she slipped out of the room. "I hope you can satisfy the Sheikh better than his last bride."

CHAPTER TWO

WHAT was she going to do? Zoe glanced wildly at the open windows and the colorful gauzy curtains fluttering in the breeze. No, she couldn't escape that way.

Even if she got out safely she had no place to hide. She had learned that over the years, after her failed attempts to run away. No one would provide her with sanctuary and the desert was a deathtrap. She had barely survived the last time.

She was trapped and she needed to come up with a plan. Zoe squeezed her eyes shut as the panic swelled in her chest. *Think, think, think!*

Her mind was locked on only one thing: chastity was highly prized in a woman, and she wasn't a virgin.

The tribe had very strict rules about sex outside marriage. The men were punished, but not as harshly as the women. Zoe tried to block out the memory of the scars her female patients had from being caned and whipped.

A man like the Sheikh would demand an untouched bride. Zoe's stomach cramped with panic. She had known that before she accepted the arrangement, but had thought she would be safe once the marriage contract was signed. It had been a risk, and it had backfired.

The door opened and Zoe went still, her breath lodging in her throat. She heard the guests offering their best wishes over the jubilant music. The jumble of noise scraped against her taut nerves. She wanted to scream, to bolt, to break down and cry, but she carefully lowered her head and clasped her hands tightly.

She flinched violently when the door closed and Zoe winced at her response. She needed to please the Sheikh, not offend him.

"Would you like a drink, Zoe?" he asked softly as he slipped off his shoes next to the door.

She wordlessly shook her head. Her mouth was dry, her throat ached, and she wished there was alcohol to numb her senses. But she didn't think she could accept a drop without choking.

How was she going to get through the night? Maybe he wouldn't notice that she wasn't a virgin? Her head ached as she tried to plan. Perhaps she could fake her virginity? She wasn't sure if she could get away with that strategy. From what she had heard about her husband he was very experienced, with an insatiable sex-drive.

She heard his cloak fall to the ground. Something soft followed. Zoe couldn't help but look, and discovered the Sheikh had removed his headdress. His hair was short, thick and black.

He didn't seem any less intimating. If anything, her husband appeared even harder, more ruthless. His profile was strong and aggressive. Power came off him in waves. She was aware that this was a man in his prime.

Zoe pulled her gaze away and stared at her hands. What was wrong with her? She was not interested in the Sheikh. He could become an obstacle to her dreams of returning home.

"It was a good ceremony," the Sheikh said, his voice closer. "Short. My favorite kind."

Zoe nodded again, although *she* thought the ceremony

had been miserably long. However, she hadn't shown up late. Not that she would point it out.

But this night was going to be endless. How was she going to prevent the fallout that was sure to come? Maybe she should fake modesty so he could never get close enough to finding out if she was a virgin or not. After all, what man would admit he'd failed to bed his wife on their wedding night?

Or she could pretend to faint dead away at the sight of him without a shirt. Zoe bit her bottom lip as she considered the merit of the idea. Or she could cry. A lot. For two solid days and nights. Men couldn't stand being around a woman in tears.

Although the Sheikh might be different. He was probably used to women trembling and crying in his presence.

She heard his footsteps approaching the bed. Zoe took a gulp of air but it fizzled in her throat. She heard the faint chime of metal and discovered her bracelets clinking against each other as her arms and hands shook.

"Zoe?"

She stilled when she heard his voice. The chiming ceased. The Sheikh was right next to her. She felt vulnerable with her head down, but she was trying to be a good Jazaari bride. It was difficult pretending to be meek when she preferred to face trouble head-on.

She decided to follow her original plan. She wouldn't run away but she wouldn't sleep with the Sheikh. Fatimah was trying to play mind games again. She wouldn't fall for it. All she needed to do tonight was keep her husband at a distance. Play the reluctant and timid bride until they left for their honeymoon. Once they were out of Jazaar she could make her escape.

"Are you giving me the silent treatment already?" He

sounded amused. "We haven't been married for more than a day."

Silent treatment? She had never been accused of that before. Her problem had always been speaking her mind. "I'm nervous, Your Highness," she replied, hating how her voice cracked.

"You may call me Nadir. And you don't have to be nervous with me."

Of course she did. He had the power to destroy her life or, unwittingly, help her to create a new one. She gave a tilt of her head to show that she understood him, and immediately tensed when he knelt on the mattress in front of her.

The bed suddenly felt smaller. *She* felt smaller as Nadir towered over her. Zoe kept her eyes firmly on her fists that rested on her lap. She watched cautiously as he reached for her hand. She jerked when she felt a hot spark between them as his skin touched hers.

Nadir's hand was dark and large against hers. Zoe felt his latent strength as he gently uncurled her fingers. She watched as he quietly slid the stack of bangles from her wrists and over her hand. She noticed how much lighter her arms felt as the bracelets fell onto the floor.

Once he'd removed her bracelets Nadir lazily traced the henna pattern on her hand with a fingertip. Her skin tingled as the pulse skittered in her wrist. Zoe was tempted to pull away.

"Your veil looks heavy," Nadir said softly.

He had no idea. "Yes."

Nadir skimmed the top of her head with his hands. Zoe's muscles tightened as she fought the urge to bolt. His gentle touch felt like a silent claim that she didn't want to accept or obey. She wanted to retreat. Brush his hands aside. Get away from the bed. Her skin prickled, heat sizzling through her blood as she struggled to remain still.

She heard the beat of her heart mingled with her short, choppy breaths. She felt Nadir guide his hands along the jeweled edge of her veil. He located the hairpins anchoring the veil and slid them free. Tossing the pins onto the floor, he glided the veil off her head and let it fall behind her.

She immediately felt its loss. While Zoe was grateful to shed the weight, the veil had allowed her to hide. She no longer had that luxury.

She kept her head down as Nadir threaded his fingers through her long brown hair. She couldn't tell if he was fascinated or disappointed by the unusual shade.

"Look at me, Zoe."

Her pulse gave a hard skip. She wasn't ready to look at him. With more courage than she'd thought she possessed, she slowly, jerkily, raised her head to meet Nadir's gaze.

Heat bloomed inside her when she saw the desire in his eyes. He lowered his head and her eyelashes fluttered. Zoe knew she should turn away but she remained motionless. She didn't know if she was relieved or disappointed when she felt his lips brush along her forehead.

Her lips stung with anticipation as Nadir skimmed his mouth along her cheek. His warm breath wafted over her skin before he placed a trail of soft kisses on her jawline. His hands were tangled in the mass of her hair, and she felt his fingers tighten when she gave a small sigh of pleasure.

Zoe leaned in closer and immediately stopped. She'd almost given herself away. She was supposed to be a bashful virginal bride. She needed to shy away, not participate!

Why was she responding so eagerly? She shouldn't soften from a few tender caresses. Was her body greedy for a man's touch because it had been so long? Or did Nadir know how to touch a woman and make her forget her best intentions?

She wasn't going to fall for this. Obviously he wanted

her to become used to his touch. He wanted her to welcome his advances and not see him as a threat.

It was too late. Nadir had been a threat from the moment he touched her. She didn't think she had ever longed for a man's touch, hungered for a kiss, as much as she did at this moment.

Her defenses couldn't crumble. She would not let him get too close. Her future depended on it.

Nadir cradled her face with his hands and covered her mouth with his.

Wild desire exploded inside her. It rushed through her veins and she melted against him. She had never been kissed like this before. Nadir's kiss claimed. Dominated.

She couldn't surrender to him. She couldn't let him find out the truth about her. Zoe knew she shouldn't let this seduction continue, but somehow she parted her lips and allowed him to thrust his tongue deep into her mouth. She returned the kiss and was instantly swept away.

Sensations overwhelmed her and she clung to Nadir's shoulders. Her hands crushed the luxurious fabric of his *dishdasha* and she drew him closer. She wanted more, so much more.

Zoe ignored her growing sense of alarm until she heard Nadir's groan. She couldn't tame the instant attraction that had flared between them. Nadir was too sensual, too dangerous. She broke the kiss and turned her head away swiftly.

She felt Nadir shudder as he tried to harness his emotions and knew she was pressing her luck. The last thing she wanted to do was frustrate him. "I'm sorry," she whispered as she looked away.

Zoe pressed her fingertips against her swollen lips. Her breasts felt heavy and there was a delicious ache low in her belly. She had to get out of this bed. Now.

As she battled back the hunger Zoe realized she had not anticipated this fatal flaw in her plan. She'd never thought she would desire the Sheikh. That he would tempt her to throw caution to the wind.

She had to be careful. This was becoming a very dangerous game. She had to hide her shameful attraction and she could not act on it. Under no circumstances could she allow him to get any closer. No more kissing!

"It's all right," he murmured. He slowly kissed down the length of her throat. "I want you to kiss me back."

That was the problem: she wanted to do more than kiss. Only she had to appear untutored and modest, Zoe reminded herself as Nadir removed her necklaces one by one. And when she kissed him she felt untamed. How did he have that much power over her responses?

She felt his hands travel down her spine and her top sagged open. Zoe's heart lurched. He had found the fasteners hidden under the beading in the back. This wedding night had gone further than she wanted and she wasn't sure how to stop it. Nadir pushed her top down her shoulders, revealing a thin white chemise.

She felt his heated gaze on her. She shivered as a dangerous excitement swept along her body, but she knew she should be feeling exposed and uncertain. What would a virgin do? Zoe belatedly crossed her arms to hide herself, but Nadir grasped her wrists.

"Don't," he ordered in a gruff voice. He lowered her arms. "Never hide yourself for me. You are beautiful."

Zoe wanted to believe that the compliment fell automatically from Nadir's lips, that he said it to all his lovers, but she felt beautiful. Desirable. Wanted. She hadn't felt like that for a long time. She had to be very careful and *not* follow her instincts, but the blood was roaring in her veins.

Nadir dipped his head and captured her mouth with his.

This time he wasn't as gentle. She fed off his aggression. His kiss was hard and hungry. He couldn't hide how much he wanted and needed her.

Heat swirled inside her. She was caught up in the kiss as he slowly lowered her. She speared her hands into his thick hair as he laid her on the bed. She'd accept one more kiss and then she'll pull away. One more…

She didn't protest when Nadir stripped her heavy skirt from her hips. He tore his mouth from hers and knelt back. She watched dazedly as he yanked off his *dishdasha* and tossed it on the floor.

Zoe gasped when she saw his golden brown skin and muscular physique. Okay, new rule, she decided frantically. No more taking off clothes. This was as far as they could go.

Without thinking she reached out and stroked his chest. She rubbed her fingertips in the sprinkle of coarse hair. She enjoyed the rasp of friction and imagined his chest, hot and sweaty, pressed against her soft breast.

She bucked her hips as the ache in her pelvis intensified. *Uh-oh.* She shouldn't have done that. Had Nadir read anything from that shameless move?

Zoe hesitated, her chest rising and falling. She needed to hide her bold responses—a virgin would be shy and uncertain. She couldn't let Nadir know how much she enjoyed exploring his body.

"Touch me again," Nadir said in a hoarse whisper. "Touch me as much as you want."

He shouldn't give her that kind of encouragement. If she touched him as much as she wanted she would not stop touching him. She would touch this legendary playboy in ways that would shock him.

But she shouldn't refuse him. Okay, revised new rule. She wouldn't go past his chest. That was safe. Zoe splayed her fingers and caressed his arms and shoulders. She smoothed her hands along his back before trailing her fingers back to his chest.

Nadir's muscles bunched as she scored his nipple with her fingernail. She hid her smile as a sense of power poured over her. She drew her hands down to his rock-hard abdomen before she reached the waistband of his white boxer shorts.

There must be something in her eyes. Something that gave away how she felt. She saw Nadir's expression tighten and the fire glow in his eyes before he swooped down and claimed her mouth again. The long, wet kiss took her breath away.

She didn't mean to part her thighs when he nestled his hips between her legs. Zoe knew he was trying to go slow and she didn't think she could slow him down further. His muscles shook with restraint as he caressed the length of her leg.

Nadir deepened their kiss and cupped her breast. Zoe was surprised by his possessive touch. It felt good. It felt right. It was all she could do not to arch into his hand. Her nipple tightened under his attention, her breasts full and heavy.

She shouldn't allow this, Zoe thought dazedly. But she was still partly clothed. She wasn't too close to the point of no return, but she was far away from her original plan. She should stop this now, no matter how much she wanted it.

Zoe gasped, the sound ringing out into the room, as he pinched her nipple between her fingers. Intense pleasure spread under her skin like wildfire. She wiggled under his body and demanded more from his kiss.

Nadir didn't follow her insistent silent command. He pulled away and she whimpered. His gaze focused on her shoulder as he pushed down the chemise strap. She felt the tremor in his hand as he peeled the fabric from her small breast. She thought she heard a purr of satisfaction before he lowered his head and took her breast into his mouth.

Zoe's moan staggered from her throat. It didn't sound virginal at all. She tilted her head back as hot pleasure poured through her. She closed her eyes, unwilling to reveal how weak and needy she felt. Nadir seemed to know exactly what she wanted. She felt the strong pull all the way to her core.

She instinctively wrapped her legs around his lean waist and drew him closer. When she felt his rock-hard erection against her flesh she realized she was in the danger zone. She wanted him inside her so much, but he would find out the truth about her.

She quickly dropped her legs as panic swelled in her chest. She grabbed his wide shoulders and tried to push him away, but he was too strong. "We've gone far enough," she blurted out. "I am *not* sleeping with you!"

She clapped her hand over her mouth. Taut silence pulsated in the room. Nadir didn't move, but she felt the ripple of tension in his body.

Now she'd done it. Zoe hunched her shoulders and waited for the explosion that was sure to follow. There was virginal reluctance and then there was outright refusal. The Sheikh was going to cast her back to her family before the night was over.

Nadir shuddered as he tried to hold back. He wanted Zoe badly. He was willing to change her mind. Lie. Cajole. Beg. He needed to taste her, sink into her wet heat and make her his in the most basic, primitive way.

He didn't understand this white-hot instant attraction, but he wasn't going to question it. It was an unexpected bonus to be attracted to his arranged bride, and he was willing to make the most of his good fortune for a few nights before he sent her away.

But Zoe didn't see it that way. Was she frightened by the unfamiliar sexual feelings or was it something else? He wondered if she had heard the rumors about him. They would send any bride into a panic.

"Zoe." He reached out for her but stopped when she flinched. Did she think he was going to hit her?

"I'm sorry," she said behind her splayed hand. "I didn't mean to say that."

"Yes, you did." He watched her expression closely. She was thinking fast, as if considering her best option.

"Okay, I did," she admitted as she dropped her hand. "But… But…you have to understand. I don't know you."

He braced his arms on the mattress and met her gaze. He sensed that wasn't her main concern. There was something false about her behavior. "I'm your husband. That's all you need to know."

Her mouth drew into a firm line and he knew she was choosing her next words carefully. "I don't know anything about you," she clarified.

That wasn't what she really wanted to say. Her eyes were very expressive. She had already made up her mind about him and it wasn't favorable. "I don't know anything about you, either," he said, "but I'm okay with that."

Zoe's eyes narrowed. "Women are different that way."

Nadir exhaled sharply. It was true. Sex wasn't just sex with women. It was a connection. It was about intimacy. And with a virgin it was supposed to be a magical experience. A sacred rite of passage.

Damn these virgins. They had to make a simple pleasure so complicated.

"In all honesty," she continued softly as she looked

away, "I don't know anything about you other than your name."

Which she hadn't used yet, he noted. He'd had visions of her crying out his name over and over, but that wasn't going to happen tonight. Nadir reluctantly slid the delicate strap of her chemise up her arm and settled it securely on her shoulder.

"I don't know your favorite color or your favorite drink."

The words rushed past her reddened lips as she tried desperately to explain herself. But he didn't believe a word of it. Zoe was trying to build barriers.

"I don't know your pet peeves or your goals. It's kind of hard to sleep with a stranger even if you are married to him."

"Women have been in arranged marriages for centuries," he argued as lust continued to scorch through his veins. "It's normal. It's natural."

"Not for me!"

Nadir gritted his teeth. An American virgin was probably the worst of the lot.

In fact his bride was very American. How long would it take for her to see the same Western sensibilities and spirit in him? If she suspected that he wasn't as conservative as he pretended she could use that against him. He needed to stay on guard around Zoe.

"Now I've made you angry," she said as her bottom lip wobbled.

Was she going to cry? Nadir rubbed his face with his hand. He hadn't even raised his voice. How would she react when he wasn't on his best behavior?

He knew she wasn't just a virgin whose expectations were different. He understood this was an emotional day for her. She was obviously coming to terms with the fact that she was married and in bed with The Beast.

That wasn't good. She was too nervous to be seduced into a sensual honeymoon, and despite what she thought he wasn't going to force her.

The last thing he needed was a bride who was scared of him. That would encourage more questions and rumors. He needed to show the tribe that he could tame this American wildcat into a traditional Jazaari woman. Once they left the village he would send her away. But for now it meant he had to be more attentive. Patient.

But he was not a patient man. He had got where he was today by being merciless, intimidating and unyielding. That strategy wouldn't work on his trembling wife. He needed to romance her. Show his tender side.

If only he had a tender side.

"Zoe, I'm not angry. Just stop cowering."

She inhaled sharply. "I don't cower," she shot back.

Ah, those tears were fake. She wasn't above using that age-old feminine technique, Nadir realized as he rose to his knees. That was good to know.

"You make a valid point about how we are strangers. We need to learn about each other more."

She nodded fiercely and relief shone brightly in her eyes. "Exactly."

"But you're still sharing a bed with me," he announced. He saw the hunted look on her face as he settled onto the other side of the bed. "How else will we know each other more?"

"I—I—"

Her gaze shifted from one point of the room to another. He knew she was trying to come up with an argument.

They had to sleep in the same bed. All it would take was one servant to notice their separate sleeping arrangements for gossip to spread like wildfire. That was the last thing he needed the tribe elders to discover.

"I won't touch you until you're ready," Nadir said.

Zoe's jaw shut with a snap. She narrowed her eyes as if she was trying to find some hidden loophole in his words. That offended him. Why should she question his word? He was a sheikh. He was her husband.

"I don't need to force myself on a woman," he said with lethal softness.

Her face paled. "I n-never said…"

"I know." She didn't have to. The look in her eyes indicated that she thought he was the fabled beast who would devour her in her sleep. Nadir swallowed back another deep sigh and turned off the lamp. "Go to sleep, Zoe."

She gave a huff, as if to say that it would be impossible. Nadir watched as she scooted off to the far edge of the bed. She lay on her side, facing him, as if she had to keep an eye on him.

"You flatter yourself," he muttered, and reached for her. She protested with a squawk, her muscles locking as he curled her against his side. He tried to ignore how well she fit against him.

"You said you wouldn't touch me until I was ready," she said stiffly.

"I won't have sex with you until you're ready," he amended. And they would have sex very soon. He would make certain. "But you're not going to get to know me, be comfortable with me, if you're hanging on the edge of the mattress."

She didn't fight out of his loose embrace, but he could tell she wanted to. Zoe would probably leave the bed the moment he fell asleep. He had to build a quicker rapport between them, but how could he do that without sex?

He looked up at the ceiling as he considered possible alternatives. He remembered what Zoe had said and he rolled his eyes. It was ridiculous, but he might as well give it a shot. "And it's blue."

"What is?" she asked.

"My favorite color," he answered gruffly. "A deep sapphire-blue. The color of the desert sky right before night falls."

The silence stretched between them. "Blue is my favorite color, too," she reluctantly admitted.

"Imagine that." Nadir didn't know if she was saying it to please him or if it was the truth. It didn't matter as long as she'd learned a little bit more about him. Tomorrow she would accept—no, *welcome* him in her bed. And then he would tame his wife with one night of exquisite pleasure before sending her away.

He closed his eyes, his body still hard, his blood racing as he inhaled Zoe's scent. Her long hair spilled over his shoulder and her soft body pressed against his. They were skin to skin.

And he couldn't do anything about it.

He hadn't expected to suffer like this, but it was a hell of a lot better than his last wedding night.

CHAPTER THREE

ZOE woke up with a violent start. Her heart banged against her chest as her muscles locked so hard they ached. She tilted her head up like a small animal scenting danger. Sunlight streamed in the windows and she heard the muted chatter of people in the courtyard. She cautiously looked to her side, praying that Nadir hadn't been watching her sleep, and found the bed blessedly empty.

She brushed her tangled hair from her eyes, finding it difficult to believe she had fallen asleep. She wanted to blame it on exhaustion and stress. It wasn't because she'd started to take Nadir at his word! All night she had lain uncomfortably in Nadir's arms. Not only had it felt strange to share her bed, but it had been a challenge to keep her hands to herself. She had been inexplicably tempted to explore Nadir's muscular body.

Zoe bolted out of bed and went straight to the bathroom. She saw some of her clothes hanging in the closet and grabbed a mustard-yellow caftan. Passing by a mirror above the sink, she caught a glimpse of her reflection and stopped.

Oh, my goodness. She shoved her hands in her tousled and wild hair and stared at her smeared make-up. She saw the outline of her body through the thin chemise. She looked bold and sexy, as though she just returned from a night of debauchery. Considering Nadir's legendary sex-drive, it was something of a surprise that he hadn't bedded her last night.

Why hadn't he? Nadir had to be up to something. Men were like that, she decided as she started the shower. They promised to love and take care of you, but really they were using you.

But this time she was using a man, she thought with dark satisfaction as she stepped into the shower stall. She was taking advantage of her husband.

As the hot water pounded against her tired body Zoe reviewed her plan. She wasn't allowed to travel at all unless she was accompanied by a male relative. It didn't matter that she was over eighteen, and it didn't matter that she was an American citizen. The law here was the law. But once she got through the third day of wedding ceremonies she would go on her honeymoon with Nadir. The moment she passed the borders of Jazaar she could escape to Texas.

She needed to find out where they were going on their honeymoon, Zoe decided as she grabbed for a washcloth. She hoped it was somewhere close to America. Once she got home—her real home—she could complete her education and live her life on her terms.

Zoe looked at her hands, which were still decorated with henna. Of course she would still be married to the Sheikh when she arrived in America, but she could get that annulled if Nadir didn't do it first. He wouldn't come after her once she reached Texas. He had his choice of women. She was interchangeable to a man like Nadir.

After Zoe got dressed, she glanced in the mirror before stepping into the living area of the hotel suite. She had done everything she could to look plain and dowdy. Her brown hair was still damp and pulled back severely in a tight braid. Her face was free of make-up and she wore no jewelry. Her faded caftan did nothing for her figure, and the shade of yellow made her skin look sallow.

Nadir was going to be horrified—but that was a good thing, she reminded herself as she quietly entered the room. If he didn't find her attractive he wouldn't rush her into bed.

She saw two servants carrying trays of food and found Nadir sitting on the silk floor pillows near the low table. Her heart gave a flip when she saw he wore a gray short-sleeve shirt and dark trousers. He rose fluidly when he saw her. She didn't realize he was speaking on a sleek cell phone until he swiftly disconnected the call.

Nadir frowned as he studied her appearance. She knew that look. Displeasure. Disapproval. Disappointment. Zoe wondered if he already had buyer's remorse.

"I hope you slept well," he finally said.

"I did," she lied. "Thank you."

His dark eyes gleamed and she assumed he knew the truth. He knew she had been on alert all night. Every time she had thought it safe to move away his hold had tightened.

"Please, have some breakfast." He gestured at the low table that was laden with food. She inhaled the aroma of strong coffee and savory breakfast dishes.

But she wasn't used to the luxury of eating first thing in the morning, and the idea of sharing a meal with Nadir felt too intimate. "No, thank you. I don't eat breakfast."

"You didn't eat much last night," he said, and he placed his hand on the small of her back. The unexpected touch startled her and she flinched. Nadir frowned as she automatically stepped away. "I insist you have breakfast."

She was surprised that he had noticed her lack of appetite. What else did this man see? She needed to stay on guard, Zoe decided as she reluctantly moved to the opposite side of the table.

"No, Zoe, sit next to me." He pointed at the large silk pillow they would share.

Zoe's gaze flew to his face. She saw a flicker in his eyes before he banked it. His expression was polite and innocent. She knew better. He was playing the role of besotted husband.

She glanced at the servants, who now stood several feet away from the table, ready to assist when needed. Zoe wondered if this display was for them. Did Nadir think the servants would gossip about their behavior? That the tribe would analyze everything including how close they sat during meals?

Or was this act simply for her? He had a reluctant bride on his hands. What better way to woo her into his bed than by playing the tender and thoughtful husband? She didn't think the act would last long, but he was going to be on his best behavior and she needed to use it her advantage.

Zoe gritted her teeth. She should never have complained about how little they knew each other. Would she be expected to stay at his side for the next couple of days?

She knew this was not a battle she wanted to fight and quietly sat down. Nadir sat next to her, his arms and legs brushing hers. She didn't like sitting this close to someone, especially a man. After years of dealing with her uncle's temper she preferred to be more than an arm's length away from any male.

She reached for the coffeepot like a drowning man would grab for a life preserver as Nadir tore off a piece of flatbread. He scooped up some mutton with the flatbread and held it out to her. Zoe gave him a questioning glance.

"Eat this," he said.

"There's plenty of food." She motioned at the bowls

and plates that covered every inch of the table. "I don't need to eat yours."

"I want to share this with you," he explained softly as he grazed her lips with the bread. "Eat."

It was not easy for her to comply. Eating from Nadir's hand required a level of trust and acceptance from her. She opened her mouth slightly and he popped the morsel in.

Zoe closed her mouth too quickly and caught the edge of his thumb. Nadir took the opportunity to stroke her bottom lip with the side of his thumb as she struggled to swallow the food.

Was he doing all this as an excuse to touch her? Why would he when she looked jaundiced? She was suddenly glad there were servants in the room, knowing that any intimacy Nadir planned would be curtailed.

Or was he trying to get her to depend on him? Did he think that if he fed her she would develop the belief that he provided for her? She couldn't figure it out, but she knew not to trust this attentive side of Nadir.

"It was a pleasure meeting your brother at the ceremony," she lied with a smile. The man had made it clear she was unworthy to sit in the same room with him. "Will he visit us today?"

"No, Rashid has already returned to the palace. He sends his regrets."

Sure he did. It was more likely that Rashid couldn't stand the idea of her marrying into the family. "Do you have any more brothers and sisters?"

"No, my mother died while giving birth to Rashid. It's just me, my brother and my father."

"Will your father attend the last ceremony?"

Nadir shook his head. "My father is unable to make the journey."

"I'm sorry to hear that. When will I meet him?" Zoe frowned when she saw Nadir hesitate.

"That's hard to say," Nadir didn't meet her gaze. "The Sultan is unwell and is not receiving visitors at this time."

Zoe's eyes narrowed. She got the feeling that Nadir didn't want her to meet his father. Was he ashamed of the match? The possibility stung.

"I forgot to ask you," she said hurriedly, changing the subject as she grabbed her coffee cup. "Where are we going on our honeymoon?"

He paused and returned his attention to his plate. "To my home in the mountains."

Her fingers clenched on the coffee cup. She was surprised it didn't shatter in her hands. "Oh," she said on strangled breath.

They weren't leaving Jazaar? No, no, no! That wasn't part of the plan.

He scooped up another chunk of mutton with a piece of flatbread. When he held it out to her his eyes narrowed on her face. "You're disappointed?"

"I'm sure it's a lovely home," she said in a rush. She couldn't afford to offend him. "I just assumed we would go overseas because you travel so much."

"The traveling is part of my work, not my private life." He held the bite of food against her lips. "I would never take my wife with me on business trips."

"Oh." She cautiously accepted the food as her mind went into overdrive. His decision ruined everything!

Nadir tilted his head as he studied her face. "You want to go somewhere?"

She hurriedly chewed and swallowed the mutton. This was her chance. She couldn't blow it. "Well, I haven't been anywhere for a while. I'd like to do some traveling."

"Do you have a place in mind?"

She shrugged. She needed to appear casual even as nervousness bit into her chest. "Europe. Australia. Maybe America."

He frowned. "But you're from America. That couldn't be of much interest to you."

"America is a big place," she replied as she took a sip of the hot, bitter coffee. "There so much of it I haven't seen."

"Why would you want to travel?" he asked as he took a bite of his breakfast. "What would you do?"

Escape. Study medicine. Reclaim the life that should have been hers.

"I'm sure there would be lots of things that would interest me."

"You're not ready to represent Jazaar," he declared as he took a pitted date from the fruit platter. "The future Sultana must be the ideal Jazaari woman and demonstrate those values."

Beauty, refinement and obedience. Zoe closed her eyes in defeat. Of all the days to dress down. Damn it.

Nadir chuckled as he held the date to her mouth. "Like I said, the outside world is not ready for a sheikha like you."

Zoe's eyes widened in horror. Had she cursed aloud? It was getting worse and worse. She automatically parted her lips to accept the date. "Didn't I look like the perfect Jazaari bride at our wedding?"

He shook his head. "I knew the truth the moment I saw you."

She hoped not. But if she couldn't convince Nadir that she was a beautiful and obedient wife, she wasn't going to get out of this country. "I can meet your expectations. All I need is a new caftan and a better pair of sandals."

He gave her a disbelieving look before he studied her yellow caftan. "Is that all you have to wear?"

"I have my wedding gowns. Why?"

"You'll need some more clothes," he said as he offered her another date.

She accepted the fruit and chewed furiously. "Are you considering a trip?"

"No, but you need to wear something befitting of a sheikha." He looked at her caftan with distaste.

It was hard to remember she was a sheikha when just a couple of days ago she'd been scrubbing floors. "There aren't that many shops in the village."

"We'll take my helicopter to Omaira."

Her eyes widened and her pulse skipped a beat. Omaira was the biggest city in Jazaar. It was a metropolitan center that she had heard rivaled Marrakesh and Dubai. Chances were there was an American embassy. She could escape Jazaar and request sanctuary the moment she stepped into the government building.

"Let me know when you want to go."

She set down her coffee cup with a clatter. "I'm ready now."

This was not one of his better ideas.

Nadir had learned quickly that he needed to watch Zoe like a hawk as they explored Omaira. His wife was endlessly fascinated with the city. She had immediately requested a map even though he could reveal any secret of the place. She insisted on asserting her independence, constantly getting lost in the dark alleys and winding streets the moment he turned his head.

Zoe was facing the excursion with startling intensity. She had craned her neck to study the architecture and stared at the red clay that edged up to the deep blue ocean. She was thrilled by the activity in the ancient marketplace, enjoying the spices and food. She was enthralled with the stores and the people.

She was interested in everything and everyone but him. In fact she seemed frustrated that he was protectively at her side and didn't allow her to venture far.

Didn't Zoe know that a good Jazaari bride focused all of her attention on her husband? Perhaps it was time to go back to the village where there weren't as many distractions? Or was she so shy with her arranged husband that she was using the city as an excuse to keep busy?

No, that wasn't it. Zoe was stubborn and disobedient, but never shy. If she grew quiet she was up to something. He already knew that much.

She tilted her head and took a few steps back to peek at a dark alley. Nadir slid her arm through his and held her firmly. "This way, Zoe."

"I can walk on my own," she replied as her fingers curled in a fist. "You act is if I need to be on a leash."

"Don't tempt me." At first he had thought she was overwhelmed with the noise and the crowds. He had thought her rebellious streak was overcompensating for her lack of sophistication.

But he'd discarded that possibility when she'd got lost for the fifth time. Her sense of direction couldn't be that poor. Nadir couldn't shake the feeling that she was *trying* to get lost. Trying to run away.

"Ah, here we are." He stopped at the entrance of a modern steel and glass building.

Zoe tried to act nonchalant as she removed her hand from his hold. She glanced at the window displays. "A jewelry store?"

Nadir fought back a smile. No woman in Jazaar would describe it as such. Paradise, maybe heaven, but never just "a jewelry store." "Fayruz has been the royal jewelers for decades."

Zoe wasn't impressed. "Why are we here?"

"You need a few things." He had noticed in the morning light that the necklaces and earrings she'd worn for her wedding were paste. Her bangles were cheap metal and the rubies and diamonds were fake. It surprised him that her family would send her off with no real jewelry. Her jewelry collection was supposed to be her financial nest egg.

She dismissed the store with a wave of her hand. "I'm fine with what I have."

She obviously didn't know about her jewelry, and he wasn't going to reveal the truth to her. "Zoe, it reflects poorly on me if you don't wear jewelry. I am buying you a necklace, some earrings, and maybe a few bracelets."

She needed the basics for her new role. Normally a sheikha would wear the royal jewels, but this was a paper marriage. She would not be at his side or living with him. If he gave her a few important pieces of jewelry people would know that she was still under his protection and care.

"No, you shouldn't. You have already bought too much." She flattened her hands on her cheeks and groaned. "All those clothes."

Most women loved to get new clothes, yet Zoe had tried on each designer outfit with reluctance. She'd tried to talk him out of his purchases, but he wouldn't listen.

"You need the clothes for your new role," he reminded her.

"But they are so expensive. I could have bought medical equipment to serve all the pregnant women in the village."

"The women don't need that."

Zoe's jaw dropped. "Are you kidding me? The women in the village don't have access to basic medicine."

"Impossible. Jazaar is a wealthy kingdom. The Ministry of Health has allocated millions to the most remote villages."

"That goes to the men," she muttered. "Because the elders decide where the money is spent."

"Enough. I'm not going to discuss this anymore," he declared as guided her to the famous turquoise doors. Jewelry was the way to gain a woman's deference. He knew from experience that even the most temperamental girlfriend could be soothed by an expensive bauble.

Zoe held back. "I appreciate the new clothes…"

"Apparently."

"…but if you need to demonstrate how wealthy Jazaar is I'd rather you use the money on building a women's medical clinic for the village."

He looked intently at her earnest face. "Your village doesn't need one."

"It does. I, however, don't need a necklace."

His cell phone rang and he bit back an oath. He was in delicate negotiations with his stubborn wife and didn't need the interruption. "Excuse me. I have to take this call."

He accepted the call and tried to listen to one of his executive assistants as he watched Zoe's expression. She looked as if she wanted to chuck his phone into the traffic and continue to argue her point. Nadir knew he had caught a glimpse of the real Zoe. Finally.

Something his assistant said caught his attention. "Would you repeat that?" he asked into the phone. He motioned his apology to Zoe as he turned away from the traffic and listened to the assistant. After giving a few orders, he ended the call.

If only getting Zoe to accept his gifts could be so easy and straightforward. "As I was saying…"

He turned around and discovered Zoe wasn't standing next to him. He glanced around the sidewalk and didn't see her anywhere.

* * *

Zoe walked briskly as her heart thudded against her chest. She wanted to run as fast as she could, but that would create a scene. She needed to do more than escape. She needed to disappear.

She glanced at the streets, recognizing the storefronts and landmarks. Having spent most of the day memorizing the layout of Omaira, she had a good idea where she was. Unfortunately the American embassy was on the opposite side of town.

Nadir might have completed his call by now. He would start to look for her. As much as it went against her instincts, Zoe ducked into a store. She wanted to put as much distance between herself and her new husband as possible, but he would easily spot her on the street. It was best to hide for a while.

She looked around and realized she had walked into a bookstore. Zoe froze, but it was too late. She had already inhaled the familiar scent of books.

Zoe picked up a book from the metal rack. It had a blinding red cover, but she didn't know the author or the title. She thumbed through the pages, enjoying the sound of the paper.

"Zoe! There you are."

Damn. Zoe tensed at the sound of Nadir's voice. He'd found her already. She had squandered her best chance of escaping.

She sensed Nadir surging forward and he was suddenly at her side. As he towered over her head she felt his frustration and chafing temper.

If she'd been facing her uncle she would have known to hunch her shoulders to protect her ears and wait for the stinging slap. Being in public and having witnesses meant nothing. Experience had also taught her that ducking out of reach only made Uncle Tareef angrier.

But she couldn't predict Nadir's response. She was jumpy, desperate to get out range, but she forced herself to remain still as she waited for his next move.

He didn't touch her, but it felt as though he surrounded her. "I've been looking for you." He was annoyed, but he didn't raise his voice. "You need to tell me where you're going."

Zoe felt impatience billowing off him, and she had to do her best to play innocent. She had to act as though she hadn't intentionally run away from him, as though she had not tried to escape.

She kept her focus on the book and continued to stroke the shiny red cover with her fingers. The book felt sleek in her hands and the weight was familiar. She remembered how good it used to feel, having a book in her hand.

"Zoe." His voice was low and rough. "I will not be ignored."

"I'm sorry." She slowly turned to face Nadir. "It's been a while since I've been in a bookstore."

He cast a glance at the small shop, shaking his head at the glossy magazines and colorful books. "You saw this bookstore from where we were standing?"

"Yes," she lied through clenched teeth.

Nadir slowly exhaled, and she suspected he was drawing on the last of his patience. "You could have gotten lost. Again," he said with calm control. "Stay with me and I won't let anything happen to you."

She pressed her lips together, not trusting herself to speak. The idea that a man would be there when you needed him the most was a fantasy. She'd learned long ago not to rely on anyone.

"Is that what you want?" He nodded at the book in her hands.

Her grip tightened on the book. Zoe sighed with regret and reluctantly replaced the book. "No."

"Pick a book. Pick a hundred of them," Nadir suggested as he gestured at the bookshelves.

From the corner of her eye Zoe saw the bookseller approaching. She dipped her head. "That's very generous of you, but it's not necessary."

He inhaled sharply and rubbed the back of his neck with his hand. "Why are you refusing every gift I offer?"

Was that what he thought? She had to tell him the truth, no matter how much it embarrassed her. "I can't read these books," Zoe whispered as her face burned red.

Nadir stilled. "You can't read?"

She jerked her head up and tilted her chin. "I can read! I love to read. But I can only read English."

His gaze held hers for one charged moment. He dragged his attention away to greet the bookseller smoothly and assure him that they were only browsing. He waited until they were alone until he said quietly, "Didn't your uncle send you to school?"

"No." She could recite all the made-up reasons she normally used when anyone asked her that question, but today she didn't feel like playing that game. "I don't want to talk about it."

"I'm sure he had a very good reason," he said.

"I'm sure." She crossed her arms tightly. Uncle Tareef had thought he had a very good reason. He'd enjoyed using her thirst for knowledge as a bargaining chip. He also hadn't liked how her intelligence challenged his.

Nadir looked at the shelf full of books and then looked back at her. "How did you read our marriage contract?"

Zoe winced. She might have just gotten tangled in a deeper problem. The only thing she could do was answer truthfully and hope for the best. "I didn't."

"Do you know what was included?" he asked. "Did anyone explain it to you?"

"No." She stared at her feet, not sure what would happen next. Did that make the marriage invalid? Was he going to call the whole thing off? Toss her back to her relatives?

"This will not do. You are a sheikha. You should be able to read and write in our language. I will remedy this immediately."

She watched him pull out his cell phone. "What are you planning?"

"I'm going to have my executive assistant schedule a tutor for you," he said as he tapped out a message. "By our first wedding anniversary you will read and write Arabic."

She didn't know if she should believe him. She had heard too many broken promises. How many times had Musad made promises, until "tomorrow" became "next time" and "soon" became "someday"? How many times had her uncle promised that if she was a good girl he would enroll her in school? The problem was that she was never good enough and eventually had stopped trying.

"That's very kind of you," Zoe said politely. She knew she should sound more grateful. More excited. But she wasn't going to get her hopes up. It would be easier this way if Nadir failed to deliver on his promise.

"It has nothing to do with kindness. You need these skills."

Not if her plans succeeded. With any luck she would be out of the country if and when the tutor showed up. "Thank you."

"You're welcome," Nadir said, and tapped another text in his cell phone. "Now it's time for tea."

"Of course." Zoe followed Nadir, but when she passed the threshold she couldn't resist taking a final look at the bookstore.

By this time next year she would be surrounded by books that she could read. By this time next *month*, she decided. The minute she returned home she would go into a public library and read her heart out.

She was silent as Nadir took her across the street to an elegant restaurant. Upon entering, Zoe realized that her attire was cheap and faded next to that of the other patrons. She wanted to disappear, but they were seated at the best table in the center of the room.

She knew she lacked the refinement and sophistication Nadir expected in a wife, but he didn't complain or make any snide comment. He didn't need to. She could tell from the faces of the other customers that her appearance reflected poorly on him.

She gradually forgot about her outfit as Nadir asked her about favorite books. She wasn't sure about his ulterior motive. Was he just making conversation, or was he figuring out how her mind ticked? She played along and discovered that having his attention was like a rollercoaster ride—enthralling and a little bit scary.

Zoe silently enjoyed the taste of freedom. The moment she had left the village she had felt as if she could breathe a little easier and spread her wings. Everything seemed brighter. Bolder. Zoe appreciated the audacious spirit in Omaira. She saw it in the daring architecture and in the enterprising people around her. It made her believe anything was possible, and that her dreams weren't out of reach.

She was grateful that her new husband didn't try to squash her growing enthusiasm. Usually when she was with her uncle she had to hide her interest. Protect it. Instead, Nadir nurtured her curiosity, pointing out what he knew she would like and encouraging her to ask questions. When she was with Nadir she felt as if her world expanded.

When they stepped out of the restaurant and walked

through the breathtakingly modern lobby Zoe saw Nadir turn on his phone. His frown seemed to deepen as he checked his messages.

"Is something wrong?" she asked.

He shrugged. "A business problem in Singapore."

Singapore. Her mind grabbed onto the word and wouldn't shake free. Singapore wasn't close to America, but it was far away from Jazaar. "I've never been there. I hear Singapore is quite beautiful."

"It is," he muttered absently as he tapped a key on his cell phone.

"I bet it's a perfect place for a honeymoon."

Nadir cast a quizzical look in her direction just as their luxury sedan rolled up to the curb. He escorted her to the car, and when they were both inside she saw a gift-wrapped package by her seat.

"That's for you," Nadir said as he continued scrolling through his messages.

"Thank you." She didn't want to accept another gift from him. He was trying hard to win her over, but all she felt was guilt.

She carefully tore off the ribbon. Once she had ripped off the paper she reluctantly opened the box. Zoe had been expecting jewelry. Something obscenely extravagant like a tiara. Instead she stared at a small gray electronic device with a screen. It was too big for a phone, but smaller than most computers she had seen. "What is it?"

"It's an e-book reader."

She picked up the light device as excitement bubbled in her chest. "E-book?"

"My assistant has programmed the reader and you can download books instantly. Now you may read whatever you want, whenever you want."

Whatever she wanted, whenever she wanted… Her head spun at the thought. "You gave me a library?"

He set his phone down and smiled at her. "That's one way of looking at it."

It was almost too good to be true. There had to be a catch. But she didn't want to think about it right now. After all these years of not having the opportunity to read, she now had all the books she wanted at her fingertips. She clasped the e-book reader to her chest. "Thank you, Nadir," she whispered.

His eyes flared bright when she said his name. "You're welcome, Zoe." He gently caressed her cheek with his fingertips. "Now we must go. The helicopter is waiting for us."

They were going back to the village? The idea suffocated Zoe. She had had a taste of freedom and she wanted more. "Are you sure you don't want to stay in Omaira?" she asked wistfully. "Didn't you say you had a place here?"

"I would like to show you our home here," he said, "but tradition requires us to return before sundown. The servants have already started preparations."

"Preparations for what?" As far as she knew they had no ceremonies to suffer through tonight.

"Our first full night together alone." Nadir's mouth tilted into a sexy smile of anticipation. "Tonight it will be the two of us. No distractions and no interruptions."

Zoe's breath hitched in her throat as her heart clanged against her ribs. She had wanted to hold him off for one more night, but Nadir was planning a full-out seduction.

And she was no match for a man like him.

CHAPTER FOUR

ZOE stared at the mirror with growing alarm. She sat quietly in front of her dressing table, panic clawing her chest as the two maids added the finishing touches to her transformation. She no longer looked like an innocent girl or a shy bride. She looked like a seductress.

This was terrible. How could she maintain the virgin act when she looked like this? Zoe took in a shallow, choppy breath and inhaled the spicy perfume she wore. The jasmine and incense were an invitation for exotic, forbidden sex. They were designed to tantalize, and the last thing Zoe needed to do was entice Nadir even closer.

She bit the inside of her lip and tightly squeezed her hands together as the maids' voices ebbed and flowed around her. The older women were experts in the traditional ritual of preparing the bride for her groom and they dismissed her concerns with a wave of their weathered hands. They didn't need a prudish bride to tell them how to prepare her for a man.

Zoe peeked from under her thick lashes and gave another glance at her reflection. She froze, and swore she wouldn't make any slanted looks in front of Nadir. It was too sexy, too suggestive.

Everything about her said she was ready for an endless night of sensual pleasure. She had been bathed, oiled, perfumed and made up for Nadir's desire. Zoe frowned at her reflection and shifted uncomfortably in her seat. She might as well place a shiny red bow around her neck along with a gift tag that said "Take me."

A fine tremor swept through her as she imagined what his response would be to such a blatant offer. She was sure that Nadir could give her mind-blowing pleasure, but she couldn't let that happen. Not tonight, when he might discover she wasn't a virgin bride. Probably not ever. She couldn't afford to lower her guard with any man, especially one as powerful and ruthless as the Sheikh.

If only she could acquire some kind of armor for the upcoming battle. The buttoned-up yellow gown that hid her figure was gone. She had heard Amina, one the maids, muttering under her breath about burning it. In its place was a long sapphire-blue negligee with a high slit at the side, offering a glimpse of her bare legs. But who would be looking at her legs when the clinging silk emphasized the thrust of her breasts and the gentle swell of her hips?

"The Sheikh is very pleased with you," Amina said as she brushed Zoe's long, thick brown hair.

"Mmm." Zoe didn't know how to respond to that opinion. Pleased? She wasn't so sure about that. He was patient because he wanted something from her.

"You survived the wedding night," said the other maid, Halima, as she tidied up the dressing table. "Not a drop of blood."

Zoe's eyes widened and her heart stopped. Her stomach gave a sickening twist. What were they referring to? Had they been looking for a bloodstain on the bedsheets that proved she had been a virgin? She hadn't considered that possibility.

"The Sheikh's last wedding night…" Halima clicked her

tongue and shook her head. "There was so much blood on the bed his bride had to be taken to the hospital in Omaira."

Zoe stared at the older woman, her heart pounding erratically. They were talking about a different wedding night. A different bride.

Nadir's first wife had had to be hospitalized after her wedding night? Fatimah hadn't mentioned that, and her cousin would have been eager to add that to her tall tale. There had to be something more to the story. "What are you talking about?"

Amina stopped brushing her hair and leaned forward, their eyes meeting in the mirror. "Didn't you ever wonder why he's called The Beast?" she asked in a low, confidential tone.

These women automatically assumed the worst of Nadir. Or were they trying to gather gossip? They wanted scandalous tidbits about her wedding night. Zoe narrowed her eyes. She wouldn't give them the satisfaction.

"Don't believe a word of it," Zoe warned the maids. "The Sheikh is a man of honor. A gentleman."

Halima raised her hands in mock surrender. "We didn't mean to offend."

"We thought we should warn you," Amina said as she resumed brushing Zoe's hair.

Frighten her was more like it. Zoe knew she shouldn't care. She should find it amusing or inconsequential. But she didn't. Maybe it was because she knew how gossip could harm a person. How it could destroy a future or ruin a life.

Zoe didn't know why she felt the need to set the women straight. She might be married to Nadir, but she hadn't sworn her allegiance to the man. "My husband would never harm a woman," she said with quiet certainty.

"You weren't there that night," Amina pointed out.

"No, but I was with him last night. I know what I'm talking about." But did she? Right now Nadir was on his best behavior, determined to create a bond with his bride.

As a healer for the women in her tribe, Zoe had taken care of domestic abuse victims. She'd listened to the women's stories as she tended to their wounds, but her concerns about them had fallen on deaf ears with the tribal leaders. She had also seen what went on in her uncle's house, and learned the pattern of his moods for her own safety.

Zoe didn't trust men in general, but she didn't think Nadir was violent. His actions last night alone told her that. He hadn't forced her into bed, but instead had allowed her to set the pace. A beast would take and take without consideration.

A man like Nadir would never have to raise his hand or his voice to get what he wanted.

"Don't underestimate the Sheikh," Amina whispered, her voice filled with foreboding. "You should have heard what Yusra's mother said. It would curl your hair."

Zoe rolled her eyes. "This is your source? Yusra's mother? Everyone knows that woman is a malicious gossip. I would never believe a word she said."

"But how do you explain—?"

"I don't have to," Zoe interrupted Halima. "I won't have anyone gossip about my husband, especially in my presence."

"Zoe, are you defending my honor?" Nadir drawled in English.

Zoe whirled around, her pulse skittering wildly when she saw Nadir at the door. His dark eyes glittered and an unpredictable energy pulsed in the room. Although he was resting his shoulder against the doorframe, she knew he was not feeling casual. He was tired of waiting and was ready to claim his bride.

Nadir tried to hide the satisfaction that spread through his chest as he held Zoe's gaze. He had not expected his new bride to defend his honor. It was more than he had hoped for.

But it didn't mean that she was loyal or committed to him, Nadir reminded himself as he watched Zoe hurriedly dismiss the shamefaced maids. She might be one of those rare women who didn't like gossip. Still, her response was a good start.

Or was it? She was already getting an idea of what kind of man he was. It wouldn't be long before she discovered that he was trying to balance tradition and innovation. That he was not like the men he would one day rule.

"Don't you know never to enter a woman's dressing room?" Zoe asked sharply as she crossed her arms.

"I can see why. One never knows what one might learn."

"Those maids have a tendency to repeat gossip without questioning the source. Don't worry about them."

"I wasn't." His only concern was what Zoe thought of him. She didn't believe the rumors about his first wedding night. There had been no hesitation when she defended him.

"Why are you here?" Zoe asked after a prolonged pause.

"I was beginning to wonder where my bride was," he said with a slow smile. "Night has fallen and the suite is empty. I was checking that you hadn't succumbed to bridal jitters and escaped out the window."

She gave a start. "Nonsense."

He caught the guilty flash in her eyes. She wanted to hide. Make a run for it. She'd declared that he wasn't a beast, but did she really believe that?

Nadir knew he had to tread lightly tonight. He needed to bind her to him, but not scare her. It required him to be romantic and charming while holding back the raw lust that whipped through him. He was determined to give Zoe the night of her life and not scare her with the intensity he felt. The very last thing he needed was a runaway bride.

"I'm sorry for the delay," Zoe said as she reluctantly stood up. "The preparations took longer than expected."

Nadir remained very still as he watched her slowly walk toward him. The way she looked, the way she moved, promised to fulfill his every fantasy. "The results are worth the wait," he said softly. "You are exquisite."

He watched Zoe blush from the compliment and sensed she wasn't comfortable with praise. He needed to be very careful as he sweet-talked her into his bed.

"Come," he said as he took her hand. He ignored the heat coursing through his veins from the simple touch. "Night has fallen and dinner is ready."

Zoe didn't think she was going to make it through the dinner without dissolving into a full panic attack. They were alone once Nadir dismissed the servants. They sat together at the low table, side by side. Her posture was rigid, her arms and legs close to her body, but somehow she kept brushing up against Nadir.

She needed something to interrupt them. Something to shatter this spell he was weaving around her.

"I haven't heard your phone ring," she commented. "Has everything been resolved?"

"Unfortunately, no. But I turned off the phone for the night. I will deal with business tomorrow."

Zoe's eyes widened. "You—you turned off your phone? Why?" *Why tonight of all nights?*

He gave a shrug. "I didn't want anything to intrude on our first full night together."

Zoe's smile froze on her face. "Good planning." Why did he have to be so attentive? She knew most brides would be thrilled by the gesture, but she needed something—anything—to disrupt his plans of seduction.

Her husband was incredibly charming and attentive, which made Zoe even more nervous. She barely ate, was almost afraid to move in case one of the delicate straps of her negligee fell, and she was very aware of Nadir's gaze upon her.

She wasn't used to this kind of attention. Most of the time she had been in the background, excluded and ignored. She preferred it that way. It was safer.

But now a part of her wanted to drink in the attention. How often had she met an incredibly sophisticated and sensual man? If she had met him under different circumstances, like at a nightclub or at a coffeehouse, she would have flirted back.

But this was Jazaar, and if Nadir found out she wasn't a virgin he could end this marriage with incredible ease. She knew she had to keep her distance, but her wall of icy politeness began to crack as he regaled her with stories of his travels. The man knew exactly how to lower her guard.

She understood he was a man of the world, but he was constantly surprising her with his insights. Educated in the best schools in America, Nadir was well-read and informed. Zoe discovered he had an adventurous spirit and some very modern ideas for Jazaar. She didn't always agree with his opinions, and was tempted to voice her ideas, but she still bore the scars from the last time she'd questioned a Jazaari male.

As she watched him drink from his glass goblet, Zoe wondered not for the first time why he had accepted marrying someone like her. He could have had any woman in the tribe. Why had Nadir agreed to her?

She was not in his league. It had to do with more than just social status. This man knew how to seduce a woman.

One kiss and she forgot everything. He knew it, too, so what was holding him back now?

When they were shopping in Omaira Nadir had gotten his way every time—and that was when he was on his best behavior. Zoe wondered how he would act if he faced a real obstacle. She always felt she would know a man's true character when he faced pressure. Her uncle had lashed out. Musad had placed her in the line of fire and ran. What would Nadir do?

She watched him pluck a grape from the fruit platter. Zoe was sure this man never had a clumsy moment. Her skin heated as she remembered how those big, masculine hands felt when he caressed her body.

"Taste this," he said as he offered her the grape.

Zoe pressed her mouth closed for a moment, but she knew declining would be useless. She shyly parted her lips as Nadir slid the dark purple fruit in her mouth. She closed her mouth as he stroked her lips with his thumb. The juicy grape burst in her mouth just as she saw the lust in his dark eyes.

She swallowed hard as hot desire sparked and showered inside her. Her eyelashes fluttered as she tried to hide her feelings, but it was no use. Nadir lowered his head and brushed his mouth against her lips.

The kiss was soft. Gentle. It was like the flutter of a butterfly's wing grazing her mouth. Nadir pulled away slightly and her lips clung to his for a moment. The unexpected sweetness pierced her, and she almost didn't want to move in fear of ruining the moment. Nadir waited silently for her to return the kiss.

Zoe turned her head abruptly. What was wrong with her? She'd expected an aggressive sensual assault, but Nadir had caught her off guard. She didn't know how to confront tenderness. The man wasn't a beast, but he was as sly as a fox.

She had to take control immediately. Set the pace for the night. She needed to act like a scared virgin for one more night. It would require a balancing act: she could not let things go too far and she must keep him from getting too frustrated.

Zoe stared at the dinner table, her eyes wide as her mind whirled with strategies. Her gaze focused on the fruit platter. "You should try one," she said hoarsely as she plucked a grape. She held it up to him and stalled, belatedly realizing that she would have to feed him.

It was a simple act, but the gesture of feeding him was too intimate. It held too much symbolism if the look in Nadir's eyes were anything to go by.

Nadir wrapped his fingers around her wrist and guided her hand to his mouth. His hold was gentle but firm. Zoe didn't like the way he took control, but she couldn't do anything but watch.

She frowned as he ignored the grape in her hand and lightly kissed her knuckles. If he felt the gradual tension in her fingers he didn't comment. Instead he grazed the edge of his teeth against the tip of her little finger.

Zoe didn't know if the sharp nip was a warning not to play games. He caught her next finger between his lips and suckled the tip. She struggled for her next breath as she felt the erotic pull deep within her.

Startled, she dropped the grape and let it roll onto the floor. She didn't yank her hand away; she didn't even try as she fought off the sting in her nipples and the heavy ache low in her hips.

She saw the gleam in his eyes. He knew how she was responding despite her attempts to hide it. He knew her body better than she did.

That scared her. She had to stop this. Stop him before he took over completely.

"Nadir?" she said, her voice rough as she tugged her hand. To her surprise, she easily broke from his hold.

Nadir leaned closer, his hands on either side of her, his muscular arms trapping her where she sat. He nestled his face in the crook of her neck. She curled her shoulder to fend him off, but she was too late.

She closed her eyes and swallowed roughly as he placed a trail of kisses along the length of her neck. She understood he was changing tactics, that tonight he was going slowly to lull her into submission. She should feel relieved that she wouldn't face the full brunt of his power, but this brand of seduction played havoc with her senses.

"Nadir…" She stifled a gasp as he placed a soft, gentle kiss against the sensitive spot under her ear. "We…we should—"

"Yes," he whispered against her ear, his warm breath tickling her skin. "We should."

He captured her mouth with his. His touch was a tender exploration. He leisurely bestowed small kisses from one corner of her lips to the other. By the time he darted his tongue along the seam of her mouth she automatically parted her lips and let him in.

Nadir cradled her head in his hands and deepened the kiss. The care in which he held her, the reverence in the kiss…it sparked something inside Zoe. She glided her hands up his chest and rested her fingertips against the broad column of his throat. She felt the beat of his pulse quicken as she hesitantly returned his kiss.

Her world slowly centered on his mouth. Their breaths mingled as he drew her tongue past his lips. There was something revealing about his kisses. He desired her, but he longed for her trust. He wanted her to surrender, cling to him, but that could never happen.

Nadir slid his hand down her shoulder and against her back. She didn't notice that he'd lowered her onto the pillows until her spine rested against cool silk. She tensed and Nadir tried to soothe her with the stroke of his hands.

Zoe was tempted to pull back and slow down, but they were only kissing. Their clothes were still on and they were nowhere near the bed. But she felt close to the danger zone, the point of no return.

She wouldn't let this slow seduction get too far, Zoe decided, as she speared her hands through Nadir's thick hair and drew him closer. The sound of his muffled groan thrilled her and a heady mix of power and pleasure swirled inside her.

This was how a kiss should be. Two people yielding to each other. Trusting and accepting. Zoe felt as if Nadir shared a little of his soul with each kiss, while stealing a little of hers.

She felt his fingers tremble as he curled them underneath her negligee strap. Her heart skipped a beat. Did he feel the same addictive excitement? Was he also struggling between accepting and resisting? Or was his restraint slipping?

Nadir pushed one strap down her shoulder and splayed his hand over her bare breast. His touch was undeniably possessive. Her tight nipple rasped against his palm. She arched against his hand, biting back a cry of pleasure.

Zoe saw the feral glow of passion in Nadir's eyes before he banked it. Trepidation trickled down her spine but it immediately disappeared as he laved his tongue against the tip of her breast.

A long moan was torn from her throat. Zoe clenched the back of Nadir's skull as a streak of white heat suffused her body. He teased her with his mouth and fingers and the slow fire inside her burned brighter.

Her breasts felt tight and heavy and a fierce ache radiated in her pelvis. The sound of her panting filled the air. Nadir slowly hitched up her negligee and skimmed his hand along her leg. When he boldly cupped her sex she bucked eagerly against his hand.

Zoe's mind shut down the moment Nadir pressed his finger against her slick clitoris. Tingling heat coiled inside her, winding tighter and tighter with each stroke of Nadir's finger. When he dipped his finger into her wet heat, she writhed under his masterful touch.

"That's it, Zoe," Nadir said roughly as he watched her chase the pleasure.

Satisfaction, warm and delicious, rippled from her core through her body. She tried to hold on to the beautiful moment and savor the pure sensation for as long as possible.

She went limp and sagged against the pillows. Her pulse pounded in her ears as she tried to catch her breath. She didn't hear the rustle of clothing. Her heart jolted, her muscles tightened when Nadir nudged his knee between her legs and settled in the cradle of her thighs.

Zoe shook her head as she tried to form words. "I'm not… I can't…" She felt the tip of Nadir's arousal press against the folds of her sex. Her traitorous body still pulsed with aftershocks and eagerly accepted him.

Nadir surged into her and stilled. Zoe saw him squeezing his eyes shut and the clench of his jaw. The muscles bunched in his cheek as his arms shook.

Zoe didn't think she could handle any more of this slow and gentle lovemaking. She instinctively tilted her hips, drawing him in deeper. Nadir tossed back his head and it was as if his restraint snapped. She felt the rumble of his moan deep in his chest before he sank into her.

She had never felt like this before. Wild sensation built inside her with each forceful thrust. It burned hotter and brighter, searing through her, scorching her mind and pressing against her skin, threatening to burst. The satisfaction Nadir gave her was ferocious.

She wrapped her arms around him and held on to him tightly, her breasts flattening against his chest, her legs winding against his hips. She clung to him, knowing that if she shattered into a million pieces Nadir would hold her together.

The red-hot climax ripped through her as Nadir drove into her with abandon. He growled low in her ear. Zoe tipped her head back, her mouth sagged open, but no sound came as she rode out the intense pleasure.

She couldn't get enough of each savage thrust and mindlessly followed his untamed rhythm. She gulped for air, inhaling the scent of hot, primitive male. Her core pulsed and clenched around him. Nadir's muscles rippled and tightened beneath her hands. With one powerful thrust he gave a gruff cry and found his release. She felt the tautness of his body before his arms collapsed and he toppled onto her.

Silence immediately descended in the room. All she heard was hoarse, jagged breathing. She gradually became aware of the heavy tension surrounding them. The moment of pure bliss evaporated as Zoe reluctantly opened her eyes.

Her seductive lover had transformed into a dangerous man. She saw the anger and menace in his glare. He pinned her to the floor, his body still joined with hers.

Fear twisted inside her. Zoe had never felt so vulnerable. So exposed. He knew the truth about her. She could tell before he said the words through his clenched teeth.

"You were no virgin."

CHAPTER FIVE

ZOE couldn't escape. She was defenseless on her back and Nadir hovered above her. His hands were flattened on the floor, trapping her.

Her heart pounded so fiercely that it hurt. She had bared herself to him and was now unprotected. Her body still pulsed from his touch. She cautiously met his glare.

Nadir's dark mood was almost tangible. Zoe couldn't believe that only moments ago he had caressed her so gently, so lovingly.

She wanted to hide. Just disappear. She wished she could close her eyes, but that wouldn't save her.

She knew she shouldn't have allowed him to get this close to her. His tenderness was all pretend, and even though she had recognized his strategy she had still fallen for it. Why? Was it because for one moment she hadn't felt so alone? So unlovable?

Tears stung the back of her eyes. She was pathetic. Stupid. When would she ever learn? Men were only nice to her when they wanted something.

Nadir must have sensed her loneliness and used it to his advantage. And, like a fool, she'd let him. Her self-disgust pricked at her like a thousand needles. Now she had to suffer the consequences.

"Answer me, Zoe," he said in a low growl.

She pushed at his arms but he was too strong. "Get off," she said through clenched teeth.

Nadir scoffed at her demand. "Not a chance."

"How dare you make that kind of accusation?" she asked. Denial was the only strategy she could think of, even though Nadir knew the truth.

"That's not going to work," he said. "I know you weren't a virgin. There was no barrier or resistance. You felt no pain, and I'm sure there will be no blood to prove your innocence."

"That doesn't mean anything."

"You don't want to push your luck with me. Start talking. What made you think you could get away with this?"

Her heart was beating so hard she thought it was going to burst out of her chest. "I don't know why you would say such a thing."

Nadir's eyes narrowed. "Did you think that I wouldn't notice?" he asked as he tilted his hips against her. Zoe gasped as her body responded. "That you could hide your reactions?"

She was appalled at the way her flesh clung to him. She hated the way she felt vibrantly alive when Nadir touched her. All her senses should be on the defense, ready to fight or flee. Didn't her survival instinct tell her that Nadir could destroy her without breaking a sweat?

"Fine!" she bit out as the dread and fear threatened to smother her. Keeping up the pretense would only make things worse. Zoe sagged against the pillow underneath her. She looked away as she confessed. "I wasn't a virgin."

The silence was thick and heavy. Zoe bit her lip as coldness seeped into her bones. What was going to happen to her? What was Nadir going to do? She wasn't sure if she was strong enough to face her future.

Zoe blinked frantically as the tears threatened to fall.

"Would you get off me…please?" she asked, her voice wavering.

She felt Nadir hesitate. He wasn't going to listen, she decided. He had her cornered and it was against his nature to give her any relief. To her surprise, Nadir reluctantly pulled away and stood up.

But then, why would he want to touch her? She wasn't the perfect Jazaari bride, and she was hardly a worthy opponent. Why put any effort into intimidating her when she'd already given him the answer he was seeking?

"Do you have a boyfriend? A lover?" Nadir asked, his movements sharp and aggressive as he adjusted his clothes. "Is he still in the picture?"

She hadn't expected him to ask. Why would he care? "No," she said as she slowly sat up. But she wasn't sure if that was the truth. Musad was the past yet he still threatened her future.

"I want the truth, Zoe. I don't want any ex-lovers hanging around. You now belong to me."

Oh, she should have known. Men were all the same. Let's not consider how the secret had serious repercussions for *her*. All Nadir was worried about was his territory. Some guy had stolen what Nadir thought was his. Some guy had got to his woman first.

Zoe felt jittery as dark emotions tore at her. Destructive emotions. She needed to play it safe, beg for mercy and promise him anything. But it was as if her body rejected the idea and she was on automatic pilot to crash and burn.

"Belong? Are you serious?" she asked bitingly. She didn't belong to anyone or anyplace. No one wanted her; they only wanted to use her temporarily.

Zoe quickly pulled up the strap of her negligee to cover herself. "Why don't you give me a list of all the women you have slept with? Just so I know in case I bump into them."

Nadir slowly placed his hands on his hips in classic battle stance. "How many men have you had sex with?"

Oh, this was getting worse and worse. Zoe knew she should have bitten her tongue and listened to his ranting until he'd exhausted his anger. She just couldn't stop herself.

"How many, Zoe?" His low, raspy voice made her shiver.

"One. Just one," she said unwillingly as she rose to her feet. It had only taken one man to ruin her life. She really knew how to choose them.

"I don't believe you."

Of course. She couldn't possibly be telling the truth. Zoe clenched her teeth and righteous anger bubbled inside her. It stood to reason that since she wasn't a virgin she must be promiscuous. "Don't judge me by your standards."

A dull red flushed Nadir's high cheekbones. She could tell that he was reining in his temper. "I didn't pretend to be an innocent," he pointed out.

"You didn't have to, did you?" He was a sheikh and followed different rules. She, on the other hand, had to be as pure as snow. "But I never said I was a virgin. You assumed."

"You played the part perfectly," Nadir said and bowed his head in deference to her acting abilities. One look into her brown eyes and he had been willing to believe anything.

He had been so patient, Nadir thought with disgust as he started to pace around the room. All this time he'd thought Zoe was shy about this rite of passage. She'd seemed uncertain about how he made her feel. Almost frightened by the intense power of those sensations. He was a fool.

No, he was worse. Nadir bowed his head as he struggled with an ugly truth about himself. From the time he was in his teens he'd truly believed he was a modern man. While he was bound to his homeland, he didn't blindly follow its customs. He questioned everything, participated only in the traditions that made sense to him, and was determined to make changes in the name of progress.

Yet the moment he'd realized Zoe wasn't a virgin he hadn't felt very civilized. His primal instincts roared to erase any other claim on her. Wipe out her memories of her first lover. Obliterate the other man's existence.

Nadir inhaled deeply and rubbed his hands over his face. He was not like his barbaric ancestors. He was not going to be ruled by primitive customs or his emotions.

But his greatest challenge would be the fierce attraction he felt for Zoe. He should have stopped the moment he discovered she wasn't a virgin, but he had been driven by an uncontrollable need. He'd had to make Zoe his.

She had a past. A love-life. That changed everything. Zoe wasn't a naïve virgin he could seduce into obedience. She wouldn't blindly follow his command after a few caresses and sweet words. She would not go quietly to his mountain palace. And he didn't think he could stay away from her.

Even now he was tempted to bed her again. This time he wanted to strip her bare and have her chant his name. Possess her body and soul. She didn't need to touch him and still he wanted to press her against his chest, kiss her senseless and fall into bed.

Nadir had never thought any woman would hold this kind of power over him—especially his arranged bride. Zoe had no idea of her sexual magnetism, for which he was thankful. If she discovered the power she wielded he would be lost. He needed to master this potentially dangerous need quickly.

He stepped in front of the window and looked out into

the star-studded night. It was better if he wasn't looking at Zoe, wasn't inhaling her scent or remembering the softness of her skin while he tried to decide his next move.

Zoe wasn't a virgin. He was disappointed that he wasn't her first, but her lack of virginity wasn't a crime. Was this the reason why she kept trying to run away? Did she think he would annul the marriage and have her caned?

Of course she did. He was The Beast, after all. She probably thought he would wield the cane himself.

Maybe he could use that to his advantage? Would she behave like a proper Jazaari woman to appease him? Just until the last wedding ceremony?

He turned and leaned against the window to study her. Her hair was mussed from his fingers, her lips red and swollen from his mouth. She had one hand on her shoulder and the other one wrapped around her waist. The self-protective gesture was no use; he still remembered her sensual beauty and how her skin tasted.

He dragged his gaze to her eyes. He saw hurt and anger. And something else. Zoe held a few more secrets. The possibility burned through him like acid. Those secrets could blow up in his face. He needed to go on the offense.

"Who knows the truth about you?" The tribe might have set him up with an impure bride just to test how he would react. "The elders?"

She looked at him as if he was crazy. "Hell, no."

"Are you sure?" He wouldn't expose Zoe's secret, but it could cost him if someone else knew it.

Her eyes flashed with anger. "If they did I would have been caned and I'd bear the scars."

That was true. His chest had clenched with anguish when he'd first seen her scars and burn marks. He had wanted to hunt down those who had made her suffer and punish them without mercy. The marks on her skin were from years of brutal hardship and abuse, but they didn't come from a cane or whip.

"You realize this is a reason to annul the marriage?" he said. He fought to keep his tone impersonal. If she thought she was safe because he couldn't afford to offend the tribe, he needed to scare her.

Zoe flinched as if she had been punched. "An annulment?" she whispered as the color leeched from her face. She looked wounded. "You would do that to me?"

He wasn't going to feel guilty. "It's in the marriage contract."

Zoe's features tightened as she glared at him. "I don't believe you." She took a step forward and pointed an accusing finger at him. "You're just trying to scare me because you know I can't read it. I should have known you'd use that information against me."

He folded his arms across his chest. He had to be ruthless and he wasn't going to apologize for it. "I'm telling the truth," he said. "According to the contract, you entered the marriage on fraudulent grounds."

"What man in this century would end a marriage because his wife isn't a virgin?"

He wouldn't end a marriage because of that. The political repercussions from another annulment would be catastrophic. He felt as if he had more to lose than Zoe, but he couldn't show it. He didn't want to give her any ammunition.

"You entered this marriage with a lie." Nadir gestured at the door. "No Jazaari man would stay with a woman he couldn't trust."

"You're right." She tossed her hands up in the air with anger. "Most of the men I know don't understand the meaning of commitment."

Nadir threaded his hands through his hair and laced

them behind his head. He found it hard to breathe as heaviness lay on his chest. He knew he had to see this marriage through, but he had to wonder if that was what Zoe was betting on. Was this why she had accepted marrying The Beast? Because he couldn't risk another annulment?

Nadir studied her intently. No, if she knew why he needed this marriage to work she would have used that already in her argument. But from the look in her eyes, Zoe seemed more interested in hiding *her* reasons for marrying *him*.

"What?" Zoe asked as she broke eye contact. "What is it?"

He tilted his head as he studied her demeanor. She was holding something back. "What else are you hiding?"

She jutted out her chin. "I don't know what you're talking about. I'm not hiding anything."

Yes, she was. "Are you sure?" he asked as dread knotted in his chest and pressed against his ribs. "Nothing like a baby?"

"A baby?" She was visibly shocked. "You think I'm pregnant?"

Nadir shrugged and breathed a little easier. His accusation had shocked her. She couldn't have faked that reaction. If it wasn't a baby, what *was* she hiding?

Zoe's eyes widened with horror. "Do I look pregnant?"

"You look guilty."

"So let me see if I've got this straight," Zoe said with exaggerated care. "Because I'm not a virgin I must be a slut. And you think that because I had sex in the past I must be pregnant now?"

He raised one eyebrow as he watched her bristle with indignation. "Sex *is* the way to get pregnant."

"I'm not pregnant," she said through clenched teeth.

"And I should take your word for it?" He gestured at her. "Based on your record of honesty?"

She tossed her head back, her long brown hair cascading down her shoulders. "I'll gladly take a pregnancy test. Right now if I have to."

"Excuse me if I don't call the front desk and request a pregnancy test on the second day of my honeymoon."

"I'm not hiding a pregnancy." She flattened her hand against her chest as if she was making a pledge. "I would never do that. Not to a man or to a child."

That was one point in her favor, but it didn't mean he was going to instantly trust her. "That's very admirable of you," he said with deep sarcasm, "but you haven't been totally honest with me."

"I'm sorry that I'm not a perfect Jazaari bride fit for a sheikh," she said bitterly. "But you are no prize either."

He took a step toward her. "Pardon?"

"Why did I think you would keep your promise?"

"What are saying? I always keep my promises." Nadir cupped his hand on Zoe's shoulder. "My word is my bond."

She shrugged off his hand. "You promised we wouldn't have sex until I was ready. You seduced me tonight and you broke your promise."

He wasn't going to be blamed for that. "You could have stopped me at any time."

Zoe arched an eyebrow and pursed her lips. "We both know that isn't true."

Nadir clenched his jaw. Perhaps she was aware that he couldn't keep his hands off her. He needed to keep his distance. He didn't trust her, but more importantly he didn't trust himself.

He needed to focus on the fact that Zoe was still hiding something from him. "The only reason you extracted the promise from me was so that I wouldn't find out you weren't a virgin."

She nodded slowly in agreement. "That's true."

Her confession surprised him. Why was she suddenly so free with the truth? It made him more suspicious than when she boldly lied to him.

"You knew there was a risk that I would discover the truth," he added. "You had to have known that an annulment was a possible outcome."

"I had hoped you wouldn't discover it until after the last wedding ceremony."

That made sense. After the last ceremony it would have been almost impossible to divorce. "When I was stuck with you?"

"When we were stuck with each other," she corrected him. She bit her lip and took a deep breath. "Just give it to me straight, Nadir. What are you going to do?"

He didn't know. He needed this marriage, but he didn't trust Zoe. Even though he planned to stow her away in a remote palace, he would still be married to her.

She looked up at him, her eyes glistening with unshed tears. "Are you going to punish me for an action I made before I met you?"

She thought he was upset that she wasn't a virgin. He'd let her think that while he tried to uncover her other secrets. "It's not your right to ask me."

"It *is* my right!" Anger flashed in her eyes as she stomped her foot on the floor. "Your decision will cast my future."

"You should have thought about that before you slept with me or the man before me!"

"Really?" She planted her hands on her hips. "What would you have done in my position? How would you have brought up the subject?"

"It's a waste of time to think about," he said as he walked past the low table. "What is done is done."

The pillows by the table snagged his attention. Hell, what had he been thinking, taking his bride on the floor? It wasn't how he had planned the night.

He halted abruptly when it occurred to him. The seduction hadn't gone as planned. He hadn't used any protection.

Nadir closed his eyes and bunched his hands into fists as he fought the alarm zigzagging through his veins. There was a chance that Zoe might be pregnant with his child.

That changed everything. Even if he was ready to face the wrath of an influential tribe for annulling yet another marriage, he couldn't do that to his child.

He had to see this through and bind himself to a woman he didn't trust. His mind was numb from the injustice of it all. Deep down he knew the Fates were punishing him for the way he'd handled his first wedding night.

"Nadir, what is it?" Zoe asked right behind him.

"I'm leaving." He needed to think this through and consider his options. He already knew he would remain married to Zoe. He just wasn't ready to voice it.

"Where are you going?" she asked anxiously.

"I'll find another place to stay for the night," he said as he made his way to the door. He needed to think before he made his next move.

Zoe yanked at his arm. "You can't do that!"

He looked down at her hands covered in henna designs clenching his shirtsleeve. "Why not?" he asked dully as heavy emotions battered inside him. "Are you worried about your reputation?"

"Yes, as a matter of fact I am!" She pulled at his sleeve with urgency. "The groom stays in the honeymoon suite. If word gets out that I displeased you I'm in big trouble."

"No one would think that." The moment he said it he

wasn't sure if it was true. Zoe was part of a tight-knit tribe. By sunrise everyone would know that she was not to his liking. She was already an outcast and this development would make life incredibly hard on her.

"Nadir, listen to me." Her bright red nails sank into the soft cloth of his shirt. "You can't give me back to my uncle."

He knew sending her back to her family would be cruel.

"I won't be spared. This will bring dishonor to my uncle and he will kill me." Her voice shook. "No one will intervene. My aunts will support his decision. The tribe will encourage it."

"Honor killing is forbidden in Jazaar," Nadir said. He suspected she had been mistreated in her uncle's house. She was very young to be this cynical. Hadn't her uncle protected her? Had her relatives given her the scars and burns? He needed to know more about her past and her family life.

"That won't stop him," Zoe said. "Please, Nadir. You can't throw me to the wolves."

"Don't tell me what to do," Nadir said as he opened the door.

"You're still leaving? After everything I told you?" Zoe dropped her hands from his arm. She took a deep breath and looked away. "Are you going to annul this marriage?"

"Don't rush me," he warned her as he walked out the door. "You will find out along with everyone else at the ceremony."

CHAPTER SIX

Nadir strode to the honeymoon suite late the next evening. He had made his decision and he wasn't happy about it. His plan of action had never really changed from the moment he realized Zoe might already be carrying his baby.

He had done his best to stay away from her until now. Just as he had expected, no one had dared question his need for another room. It helped that his cell phone kept ringing. A brief mention that he didn't want to disturb his new wife with business calls and he was given another suite.

His upper lip curled into a sneer. He was almost as good of a liar as his wife.

His wife. The words sliced through him like a dagger. His deceitful, untrustworthy wife. The thought of her had kept him up all night.

Worse, he'd had trouble focusing on urgent business negotiations during the day. His mind had kept veering to the memory of her soft, fragrant skin or the way her legs had gripped him in the heat of passion. He wanted to be with her as much as he wanted to stay away.

Nadir paused as his body hardened from the sensual memory. He had to master this raw, powerful lust. The absence of his legendary willpower was not improving his dark mood. He clenched his jaw and slid the key card into the door with more force than necessary.

He needed to be in command by the time he saw Zoe. Show her that he would not be swayed by her feminine charm or tears. The night was going to be torture, knowing he had to play the happy groom but trying to keep all physical contact to an absolute minimum.

He entered the honeymoon suite and his frown deepened when he realized that his troublesome bride wasn't in the sitting room waiting for him. That was a bad move on her part, he decided. If Zoe wanted to remain married she should be ready for him, preferably meek, obedient and silent.

He grimaced as the last thought lingered in his head. Now he was sounding like his father, with his archaic ideas and outdated values. Zoe had the remarkable ability to test his ideals and drive him crazy.

Nadir turned toward the bedroom and saw Zoe's two maids. They were dressed in colorful *abayas* and headscarves. He noticed they were knocking timidly on the closed door with their bejeweled hands.

"Why are you not preparing the Sheikha?" Nadir asked as he approached them.

Amina twirled around and gasped, clutching her thick necklace with a tense hand. Halima slowly faced him, flattened her hands on the door and bent her head in defeat.

"We were adding the finishing touches," Amina said as she motioned at the door. "Then she l-led us to the door and l-locked herself in the bedroom."

Nadir didn't say anything and showed no outward appearance of concern. But he knew that Zoe wasn't coming out of the bedroom without a fight.

"She says she's not going to the ceremony," Halima added as she continued to hang her head low.

Zoe was very wrong to give such a challenge. She would

soon learn not to test him so brazenly. "You may leave," he told the maids. "I will get my wife ready for the ceremony."

Amina and Halima exchanged glances. The older women were not convinced by his display of husbandly patience.

"No need to be alarmed," he said, with a smile he didn't feel. "My wife hates ceremonies and she's not used to being the center of attention. I will take care of this."

They still hesitated.

"Please join the party." Nadir wrapped the order in the form of an invitation and gestured for them to leave. "The Sheikha and I will be there momentarily."

The maids knew a command when they heard one and scurried away. As Nadir waited impatiently for them to leave he considered the methods his father and grandfather would have used to tame a disobedient bride.

No, Nadir thought as he closed his eyes and harnessed the last of his patience. He wouldn't act like his ancestors. Zoe was a modern woman and he would behave like a civilized man.

Once the women had vacated the hotel suite, Nadir gave an imperious knock on the locked door. "Zoe? It's time to leave for the ceremony."

"I'm not going."

She wasn't near to the door. In fact, she sounded as if she was on the opposite side of the room. Yet the defiance rang clear in her voice.

Nadir suspected that he was getting a glimpse of the real Zoe. Stubborn. Unmanageable. Intriguing. "Open this door," he said with a hint of warning.

"So you can present me to the tribe, tell them I'm not worthy of you, and toss me back to my uncle? Forget it."

He didn't have time for this. There was no way he would

discuss this matter through a locked door. "This is your last warning."

"You can make the announcement without me," Zoe said. "Tell me how the party went."

Nadir took a step back and gave the door a fierce kick. He barely heard Zoe's startled yelp over the sound of splintering wood. The door flew open and crashed against the wall.

Zoe whirled, her gold ceremonial gown swishing around her. She was stunning. Nadir gripped the doorframe for support as his knees threatened to buckle.

He took a long, silent look. His heart thudded in his ears as his gaze drifted to her dark hair. It was swept up in soft waves, and instead of a veil she wore a small sparkling tiara. Zoe had been transformed into a regal beauty.

The gold caftan gleamed in the light. He couldn't help notice that the silk skimmed her body and hinted at the curves underneath. He swallowed hard and tightened his hold on the doorframe. She was magnificent. He had thought Zoe was sexy when he first saw her, but nothing had prepared him for the impact of her beauty now.

She stood defiantly before him. Her hands were curled into fists at her sides and her eyes flashed with rebellion and fear. "If you try to drag me down to the ceremony," she said in a low, fierce voice, "I will kick, scream and claw at you every step of the way."

"I have no doubt," Nadir said as if he was hypnotized. The beat of his heart slowed. He blinked hard to break the trance.

Her eyes narrowed as she watched him enter the room. "I am not going to stand beside you in front of everyone only to have you publicly humiliate me."

Nadir approached her with caution. She was irresistible

and he didn't trust his self-control. "Behave and I won't ask for an annulment."

Zoe didn't look relieved. She looked suspicious. "I don't believe you. Your mind-games won't work on me."

"I don't care that you weren't a virgin on our wedding night."

Zoe cast a quick look at the doorway. "Keep your voice down."

"I care that you are keeping secrets from me. I don't need any unpleasant surprises. For all I know, you're going to sabotage me at the ceremony."

"Right. Like I have that kind of power. Don't try to sweet-talk me. You'll say anything to get me down to the ceremony so you can have the pleasure of discarding me like garbage."

"If I really wanted to end this marriage, all I'd have to do is bring the elders up to this room and complete the necessary rituals."

She held out her hand. "Don't step any closer."

He ignored her and kept approaching until his chest reached her outstretched hand. He felt her fingers trembling. "Zoe, you will attend this ceremony and you will stand at my side looking happy and satisfied."

Zoe gave a mirthless chuckle. "That's never going to happen."

Nadir took a deep breath. "You need to understand that my last wedding caused irreparable damage to the relationship I have with your tribe."

She slowly lowered her hand. "So?"

He took the opportunity to step closer. "The elders believe that I am too Western to one day rule Jazaar. That's why they gave me you. An American bride. Many have used how I handled my last wedding as an example of my disrespect for tradition."

"So you'll be a modern leader. They'll learn to accept it. What's the big deal?"

He hesitated. Did he really want Zoe to know that he had to rely on her? She could use the information against him, but he had to get through to her.

"Zoe, they will try to destroy me in order to protect their way of life."

She stilled and cautiously stole a look at him, searching his eyes to determine if this was an elaborate lie. She didn't say anything.

"If I seek another annulment there will be serious political repercussions," he admitted.

She looked away. He could tell that she was deep in thought. Was she considering what he was saying, or was she plotting his downfall?

"Don't think of me," he said quietly. "Think about the ones you healed. The families you've taken care of and the children you have helped bring into this world. They will lose everything if they try to fight me."

He saw the struggle in her eyes. Zoe might be an outcast in her tribe, but she wasn't vindictive. She truly cared about those she helped in her community.

"You must trust me," he said roughly as emotions squeezed his chest.

She shook her head as if she was trying to clear her mind. "You've broken your promise to me before. You tossed your first wife back to the tribe, and I'm supposed to believe you won't do it again?"

He had to admit he was asking a great deal from her, but he expected nothing less from the wife.

"And now you're telling me you're going to win any conflict with the tribe." She folded her arm tightly. "You might suffer a setback, but I'm the one who will be destroyed. Nothing is really stopping you."

"And nothing is stopping me from throwing you over my shoulder and carrying you out of this room," he replied, his voice shaking with the last of his restraint.

Their gazes clashed as heightened tension shimmered between them. Nadir hid nothing from her, determined to show that he wasn't lying. He hated this feeling. He couldn't remember a time when he'd felt so exposed.

Zoe suddenly moved past him. "So help me, Nadir," she said through clenched teeth, "if you're lying to me I will kill you with my bare hands."

Relief poured through him. He grabbed her wrist as she walked past him. She jerked to a standstill. He felt her racing pulse under his fingertips. "Stay at my side and take my arm."

She muttered something under her breath. He didn't catch it under the roar of his blood. She clamped her hand on the crook of his arm and an unpredictable energy vibrated from her.

Did she really believe him, or was she setting him up for a catastrophic night? Nadir couldn't tell and he didn't like walking into a battlefield without knowing his allies and enemies.

He gently covered her hand with his. "Now follow my lead."

She refused to look at him and kept her gaze straight ahead. "Don't make me regret it."

Zoe didn't want to hold on to Nadir's arm, but she didn't think she could stay upright by herself. Her legs were shaking violently. Her body was numb as fear congealed in her stomach. She couldn't obey the instincts screaming for her to run and hide.

When a servant held the elevator for them, Zoe's body protested against moving forward. She gulped for fresh air and her muscles locked. She almost stumbled as Nadir gently nudged her.

She dipped her head, the world slowing down as she stepped into the elevator. Her heart raced and her skin flushed. When she heard the elevator doors clang shut, she jumped.

"Relax," Nadir whispered as he stared straight ahead.

Right. Relax. Did the executioner say that to the prisoner right before he wielded the ax?

Zoe closed her eyes and took in a shaky breath. She didn't trust Nadir, but she wanted to. She didn't have much practice trusting men. The idea of even trying scared her. Sooner or later they had always disappointed her. Betrayed her. Used her. Why should Nadir be any different?

Zoe nervously glanced at him, but he wasn't looking at her. She didn't know if that was a good or bad thing. She needed to see his eyes. If there was a glimmer of kindness she knew she would be all right.

"Nadir?" She hated how her voice cracked.

He glanced up at the lights that told him which floor they were on. "It's time to give your best performance."

She heard the chime and took a step back. *She wasn't ready!*

Zoe didn't think she had the strength to leave the elevator. Nadir's grip tightened on her hand. There was no backing out.

She took a deep, shuddering breath. She dipped her head and silently prayed for a miracle. As the elevator door swung open she lifted her head, pasted on a polite smile and stepped across the threshold.

The small lobby was quiet and almost empty, since many of the guests were waiting for them in the courtyard. Zoe heard light music and conversation drifting from outside.

"Zoe!" Her cousin Fatimah was standing by the bank of elevators. She was dressed in a vibrant red caftan that was designed to turn heads.

No, no, no. Zoe's smile froze on her face. She didn't need to deal with her poisonous cousin. Not now. The last thing she needed was for Fatimah to give Nadir any additional reason to abandon her.

"Many felicitations on your wedding."

"Thank you, Fatimah," Zoe said stiffly. Her cousin was *never* this happy for her.

Fatimah gave a sly look to Nadir. "And to you, Your Highness. I'm so glad that Zoe has pleased you."

Zoe tilted her head with suspicion. There was something about Fatimah's tone. She had heard it many times before. Her cousin was about to make the first strike.

"But it doesn't surprise me," Fatimah said conversationally as her eyes glittered with menace, "considering her wealth of experience with men."

Zoe froze as her cousin's condemning words flayed her like a whip. The pain consumed her like fire. She couldn't believe the depth of Fatimah's hatred. How could one woman cause so much damage with one breath?

"Fatimah, be very, very careful," Nadir said in a low voice that hinted at dangerous undercurrents. "Anything you say against Zoe, you say against me."

Fatimah faced Nadir as she would an unfamiliar opponent. "I'm not sure I understand what you mean," she said sweetly as she studied Nadir through her batting lashes.

"Then let me be clear." He didn't raise his voice, but it held a frightening quality that made Zoe shiver. "If there are any malicious rumors about Zoe, I will hold *you* responsible."

Fatimah jerked as her jaw sagged. "But that's not fair."

Nadir shrugged. He didn't care. "You've been warned.

I'm a reasonable man, but when I'm crossed I will show no mercy."

Zoe clung onto Nadir's arm as he guided her away from Fatimah and toward the courtyard.

"Fatimah will try to take another swipe at you," he murmured to Zoe, "but I have declawed her. She shouldn't be a real threat anymore."

"Thank you," she said weakly. She wasn't sure what to say or do. It had been a long time since someone had come to her defense.

His hand tightened on hers, causing her to look up at his face. There was coldness in his expression, not one hint of softness. "I thought no one knew."

Zoe tensed. She would not be blamed. "I never said a word to anyone. That would have been suicide."

"Then your lover didn't care enough to protect you," he said with brutal honesty. "And you were extremely reckless."

"Can we not discuss this right now?" she asked as the sounds of the party grew louder.

"With pleasure."

The wedding guests were waiting impatiently and greeted them with applause as Zoe and Nadir stepped onto the courtyard. Zoe desperately wanted to close her eyes and hang back. Disappear altogether.

As they walked to the dais covered with faded Persian rugs, Zoe noticed that the greeting was cautious. Were the tribe trying to determine if history would repeat itself? Panic fluttered in her chest and the sweet fragrance of the flowers choked her.

She fought to maintain her smile as she watched her tribesmen study Nadir's expression. She didn't know what they were concerned about other than money lost. They had probably placed bets on the outcome of this wedding.

She was the one who would lose her dreams, her future and her freedom.

Zoe cast a glance at Nadir. He gave nothing away. There was no smile, and yet no anger, either. His expression was somber.

He's not going to cast you back to your uncle, Zoe told herself fiercely as she got closer and closer to the dais where her fate would be decided. *He stood up for you against Fatimah.*

But that could have been a gesture of protection before she was discarded. Not that his protection would do her any good if Nadir wasn't there to enforce it.

He was going to annul the wedding. Zoe was sure of it. The fear crystallized, scraping inside her until she didn't think she could stand straight. Zoe kept her gaze on the Persian rugs as she considered her getaway.

But there was nowhere to run or hide. She'd last less than a day in the desert that surrounded the village. The only thing she could do was stand before everyone.

The music ended abruptly and the guests fell silent. Zoe went from cold to numb as she heard the familiar shuffle of the chief elder getting closer. It would only be a few moments before Nadir either claimed her as his wife or disposed of her.

Nadir needed this marriage. No, it was more than that, Zoe decided as she remembered the earnest look in his eyes. They needed to rely on each other.

Zoe's heart pounded. She wasn't sure if she was brave enough to take that kind of risk. She wasn't very good at relying on someone else.

The elder stood before them. Zoe struggled for her next breath as black dots formed around the corners of her eyes. She tightened her grip on Nadir's arm. She found it strange that she was relying on the very man whose strength could destroy her.

Her hands were ice-cold as Nadir and the elder exchanged pleasantries. When they turned their attention to Zoe, she felt as if she was going to shatter.

"Allow me to introduce my wife," Nadir said to the older man.

Her breath was suspended in her throat. She was afraid to sag against Nadir in case she'd dreamed those words. It was only when the guests exploded with cheers that Zoe knew she was no longer under her uncle's heartless power.

Now she belonged to the Sheikh.

CHAPTER SEVEN

Zoe dismissed her curious maids for the night and gave one final glance at the clock. It had been hours since the ceremony concluded. Instead of returning to the honeymoon suite with Zoe, Nadir had been invited to a private meeting with the tribe's elders. He had sent her upstairs without a backward glance.

Now that she had risked everything to stand beside him, Nadir had no use for her anymore. Good, Zoe decided as she flicked the hem of her short emerald-green negligee and walked over to the bed. She was happy with the development. Thrilled. She was tired and she didn't have to be on her best behavior anymore.

Slipping between the sheets and turning off the lamp, Zoe rested her head on the pillow and tried to get comfortable. If only she could forget the pleasure Nadir had given her last night. She needed to keep a safe distance. She knew better than to get close to a man. Rely on him. Want him. It only brought trouble.

Zoe frowned as images of Nadir and Uncle Tareef tumbled across her mind. They had spoken like friends at the ceremony, and that hurt because Nadir knew how the man had treated her. Maybe Nadir didn't believe her. After all, what man would take the word of a woman over that of another man? The word of an outcast over a respected citizen?

She needed to be cautious with Nadir. If she had problems with her uncle, Nadir would side with Tareef. She still wasn't safe or free while living in this ultra-conservative desert kingdom, but she would safer under the Sheikh's protection.

His protection was all she would get from Nadir. She was fine with that. Ecstatic. If she was lucky, he would barely pay attention to her. He had consummated the marriage and no longer needed to associate with his wife. He was probably in the second hotel suite right now, while she was aching for his touch.

Zoe moved restlessly. So what if she was in a loveless marriage? So what if she longed for a man who didn't want to share a bed with her? It was better this way. She'd get over the rejection. And once she got back to Texas she would be embraced by her old friends and wouldn't feel so alone.

She gave her pillow a punch and settled down. At least she wouldn't throw herself at Nadir out of loneliness. She wouldn't make the mistake of equating love with sex. It was a good thing she had learned her lesson with Musad, because if Nadir tried to seduce her again she wouldn't be able to resist.

She didn't have anything to worry about because he wouldn't lower himself again. She was an outcast. A bride no man wanted. She wasn't a perfect Jazaari woman. She hadn't come to him as a virgin. He wouldn't return to this bed.

Zoe curled into herself, determined to dream about a better tomorrow. It took a long time for her to relax.

Just as she started to fall asleep she felt the sheets lifted from her warm skin and the mattress sink underneath her. She blinked groggily and saw Nadir lying beside her.

Heat rushed through her veins and her heart leapt. She hated how energized she felt when she was with Nadir, but at the same time she found the sensation addictive. "What are you doing here?"

"It's my bed."

Were the shadows creating an optical illusion, or was he moving closer to her? She could have sworn he hadn't moved. "It was your bed last night but you didn't sleep in it."

"Last night I didn't know your ulterior motive for marrying The Beast."

Her breath hitched in her throat. He sounded so confident, but he didn't know everything. He couldn't. "And now you know?" she asked, hiding her vulnerability with aggression. "Or have you suddenly gotten over your raging paranoia?"

"You agreed to an arranged marriage because you needed to get out of your uncle's house before he found out about your...ill-advised romantic liaison."

If she hadn't been so nervous she would have smiled at his attempt to soften what was her biggest mistake. "Nothing gets past you. But how does this change last night? You were furious that I wasn't a virgin."

"You took me by surprise, but it doesn't matter to me if you were a virgin or not when entering this marriage."

"How modern of you," she drawled.

"You could have warned me."

"No, I couldn't."

"Last night I thought you were hiding something else. Something more serious. But your only fear was being sent back to your family. That concern is gone. Tonight you have nothing to hide."

He had no idea that she had even more reasons to hide tonight. The more she revealed herself to him, the sooner he'd learn all her secrets.

"You are in a very forgiving mood," she said. "What's really going on?"

"Honestly?" He reached for her and drew her close. "I couldn't stay away from you."

"Stop teasing. It's not funny." She pressed her hands against his bare chest. As her legs collided against his she discovered that he was naked. Dark excitement pierced her.

"You don't believe me?" he asked in a husky voice. "Let me show you."

Zoe knew she should protest and avoid him. When he touched her she didn't think about anything else. The way he made her feel was so intense that every goal and dream she had was momentarily forgotten.

Nadir covered her mouth with his. Pleasure, hot and tingly, washed over her. She softened the moment his lips touched hers. She wanted to melt into him as his kisses became urgent and demanding.

She shouldn't yield so quickly. She needed to create an emotional distance and not reveal her deepest fears and desires. It was safer that way. She must never give Nadir that much power over her.

She pulled away. "There is no need for us to sleep in the same bed. We are officially married."

"I know one way to celebrate an official marriage." Nadir pulled her against his chest and she felt the heat pouring off him. "And it requires a bed."

When he pressed his hands against the small of her back she couldn't resist tilting her hips. He murmured his delight as she slid her bare leg over his.

"This is a bad idea," she whispered as she immediately straightened her leg. "We don't have to have sex. The marriage has been consummated. It's legal. It's done. There's no going back."

"Think of this as added insurance," he suggested, his hand caressing the length of her spine.

Zoe arched, her breasts thrusting against his chest, her tight nipples rasping against the thin silk. She discovered that she really wanted to accept the flimsy excuse. She wanted to have one more night with the Sheikh.

Nadir plucked the strap of her negligee with impatience. "Take this off," he said against her mouth.

Zoe hesitated and shook her head. The more barriers they had between them, the better it was for her.

Nadir's kisses became less demanding and more persuasive. Zoe sighed as his lips lingered on hers. "You don't need to be shy with me," he whispered.

Shyness had nothing to do with it. Her first instinct was to strip off the emerald silk. But she couldn't capitulate so quickly. She wouldn't let him take over. If only she had as much power over him as he did over her.

"What if I let you set the pace?" he asked.

Zoe bit her lip as heat washed over her. "*Let* me?" she asked. "I can take control anytime I want."

"Then what's stopping you?" he challenged.

"Because you'll snatch the control away from me." It wasn't the full truth but just one of the reasons.

"Try me."

She'd love to, but she shouldn't. She wanted Nadir, but she didn't want to get too close. But it would be just one more time. How could she possibly get too attached, knowing that this would be the last time? Especially if she was setting the pace.

Zoe skimmed her hands over his broad shoulders and muscular back. She felt the strength and power under his warm skin. As she trailed her fingertips over his hip bone he jerked. Zoe smiled against his mouth at the telltale sign. She had just discovered he was ticklish. She was inordinately pleased that he had a weak spot.

She drew her hand lower, but Nadir encircled her wrist with his strong fingers. She groaned with disappointment as he moved her hand to his shoulder.

"Don't you want me to touch you?" she asked.

"I don't want this to end before it begins," he said as he skimmed the strap down her shoulder.

"We have all night," she reminded him as rubbed her fingertips along his chest. She would need all night to wrestle control from him. It would take a lifetime to hold any sexual spell over him.

Nadir looked intently into her face. Zoe held her breath. She wasn't sure what he hoped to find. The darkness was a veil, and he wouldn't be able to read her eyes among the shadows.

To Zoe's surprise, Nadir gathered her close and rolled onto his back. She was sprawled on top of him as she stared at him in confusion.

"Touch me as much as you want," he offered.

Zoe's heart started to pump hard. Her skin felt hot and taut. She wanted to explore and taste all of him, but that would reveal just how much she wanted him, how much she couldn't keep her hands off him. He would use that to his advantage.

Unless she drove him wild first. She wasn't sure if she could. She slowly straddled his legs and placed her hands on his shoulders.

"Put your hands behind your head," she ordered softly. She sensed his curiosity and added, "I don't want you to stop me."

"I wouldn't dream of it," he drawled as he laced his hands underneath his head.

She couldn't read his eyes, but she saw the arrogant smile and felt the male confidence coming off him in waves.

She wanted to rattle his confidence. She dipped her head, her long hair cascading onto his shoulders. She darted her tongue at the center of his collarbone. He tasted warm and male. She dragged the tip of her tongue from the base of his throat to the cleft of his chin. She dared a glance at his face as she deliberately licked her lips. His features were stiff, his jaw clenched.

"Do you want to stop me now?" she taunted.

His eyes glittered. "No," he answered gruffly.

A reckless fire coursed through her veins. He didn't want to show his weakness any more than she did. Zoe leisurely stroked his chest before licking and teasing his flat brown nipples with her teeth. As she caressed his abdomen she listened to the way his breath hitched in his throat and felt his muscles bunch under her touch.

She gently wrapped her hand around the base of his hard length. Nadir bucked. She pumped her hand and watched him arch his back, listened to his choppy breathing. When Zoe took him in her mouth he tangled his fingers into her silky hair.

Suddenly he pulled her up. She barely had time to protest as he grabbed her by the waist. She looked down at him, her tousled hair in her face as Nadir positioned her. She straddled his hips and he guided her down.

"I thought I was in charge," she murmured.

"I changed my mind," he said through clenched teeth. She felt the sexual energy pulsing from him. He was through indulging her.

"I knew it wouldn't last," she said in a husky voice as her breath caught in her throat.

A relentless heat flushed through her as she sank onto

his length. He slowly stretched and filled her. Zoe struggled for her next breath. She rocked her hips and a shower of pleasure sparked inside her.

Wild need lashed inside her. She wanted to close her eyes to hide how she felt, but she couldn't pull her gaze away from his.

She reached for the hem of her short negligee. Slowly she bunched the silk higher. She teased Nadir, enjoying the rise and fall of his chest as she rolled and tilted her hips. She allowed the silk to fall back down before she bunched it up higher still. As she finally stripped and tossed the negligee to the side she no longer felt vulnerable under his hot gaze. Instead she felt beautiful. Sexy. Powerful.

When his hands tightened on her hips she knew the teasing was over. He had indulged her long enough and he was taking over. She saw the primal male look in his eye before he led her into a wild, intense rhythm.

The pleasure Nadir gave overwhelmed her. Overpowered her senses. She was out of control, mindlessly following him. It was as if her body was not her own. She desperately needed to pull back even though her body begged for release.

She wanted to submit to the excruciating pleasure, but she knew the moment would change her. If she surrendered now, she would be bound to him in the most elemental way.

Nadir slid his hand against the damp curls between her legs and pressed his fingertip against her clitoris. White hot pleasure ripped through her like a bolt of lightning.

Zoe cried out as sensations tore across her mind. She couldn't hide her response. She rode the wave of pleasure as she felt Nadir find his own thundering release.

Moments later she slumped against him. Her body still pulsed, her skin was slick with sweat and she nestled her head against his shoulder. She knew it would be better, safer, if she went back to her side of the bed. But she needed to sustain the connection a little longer.

She squeezed her eyes shut as she listened to the erratic beat of Nadir's heart. If she wasn't careful she might become infatuated with her arranged husband.

That would the biggest mistake she could make. She wasn't going to trust this feeling. Nothing would keep her in Jazaar.

CHAPTER EIGHT

SUNSHINE streamed into the bedroom windows. Nadir propped his arm and rested his chin against his hand as he watched Zoe sleep. She was curled up in a ball, her fists under her pillow, her legs drawn up.

Even in sleep she wouldn't let anyone get close. He knew that wasn't always true. She had allowed one man into her heart. A man who hadn't been worthy of her trust.

Soon Zoe would learn to trust and rely solely on him. It was his right to expect complete loyalty and honor from his wife. Perhaps he would need to visit her in the mountains from time to time to reinforce her commitment. It wouldn't be a hardship to share her bed whenever he visited.

But she could never live in the Sultan's palace. She was too American, too improper to be his wife. He would have to hide her away if he wanted the political support of the Jazaari men.

Nadir brushed a wayward piece of hair from her cheek. He was amazed that someone with her harsh upbringing had such a soft exterior. Zoe's forehead wrinkled in a frown and she curled into herself even tighter.

He was tempted to stroke her gently. Coax her into opening up to him. She had last night, giving him a glimpse of the passion and fire inside her. He imagined how wild and intense the sex would be if she trusted him completely.

Nadir shifted restlessly as anticipation coursed through his veins. He wanted her again. He was becoming insatiable. Throughout the night he had reached for her. Even as they slept he had had to touch her. He couldn't remember the last time he'd felt like this about a woman. He didn't want to inspect this need too closely, certain the fierce lust would burn out once the honeymoon was over.

He had decided that Zoe had had enough time to sleep when he heard the familiar buzz of his cell phone. He hesitated for a moment, wanting to ignore his duty. He was tempted to tune out the rest of the world so he could enjoy a leisurely morning of pleasure with Zoe.

The persistent buzz of the phone reminded him that the demands of business would continue to intrude. He got out of bed quietly so he didn't waken Zoe. With the hope that he could conclude business quickly and return to bed, he strode naked to the sitting room to find his cell phone.

He grabbed it from a low table and answered with a harsh growl. His mood didn't improve as he listened to his assistant.

"I will go to Singapore and deal with it myself," he said. "Make the arrangements for me to leave tonight."

Nadir ended the call, wrestling with an unfamiliar sense of reluctance and disappointment. He didn't want to leave Jazaar. He stared out the window that overlooked the desert. These days it felt as if he was away from his beloved land more than he was home.

"You're going somewhere?"

Nadir turned when he heard Zoe's voice, husky with sleep. He saw her leaning against the bedroom door. Her tousled long hair fell in waves, hiding most of her face. She held a rumpled bedsheet against her.

"I am in charge of a business deal that's important to the future of Jazaar," he explained slowly as his gaze traveled down the sheet that barely hid her curves. His body stirred in response. "Negotiations have broken down. I have to go to Singapore."

"What about me?"

He dragged his gaze up to her face. "What about you?"

"Where am I going? You can't leave me," she said as she casually brushed her hair from her eyes. "It will look bad if the honeymoon ends abruptly."

She said it lightly, but Nadir understood her concern. Even though he had announced Zoe was his wife, it *would* look bad if he left her immediately after the wedding ceremony. It wouldn't strengthen his fragile relationship with the tribe.

Nadir knew he could quietly send Zoe to Omaira or to his mountain palace. No one in the tribe would know that they weren't together. But Zoe was still keeping secrets. What if she tried to run away again? That would shame him in the eyes of his people.

"The honeymoon hasn't ended," Nadir said as he walked towards her. "You are coming to Singapore with me."

Zoe went completely still as a tension invaded her body. "Are you serious?" she whispered.

"Of course." He rested his arm against the doorframe and looked down at her. "Why do you ask?"

She bit her lip. "You said you wouldn't take your wife on business trips."

It was true, but it was in his best interests to take Zoe with him. As he had investigated her family over the last few days he had found several reports of her defiance and disobedience. He got the feeling she would not accept being sent away quietly.

Nadir had also seen in the reports that Zoe had attempted to run away countless times. What if she was running toward something? Or someone—like her lover?

"This isn't just a business trip," he announced. "We are relocating the honeymoon."

No matter how hard Zoe tried to hide it, Nadir saw the excitement building up inside her. He didn't know why she felt the need to keep her enthusiasm hidden. The idea of traveling seemed incredibly important to her.

"This way I can keep an eye on you," he said as he tucked a long curl of her hair behind her ear.

The excitement in her eyes dimmed and she scowled. "I don't need a babysitter."

"I will be the judge of that." He trailed his hand down her throat. His fingertips rested on her pulsepoint. "Something tells me that you'll make a run for it the moment my back is turned."

Zoe lowered her gaze. "You're paranoid. Anyway, I don't have a passport," she said, her chest rising and falling rapidly. "I don't even have luggage."

"Mere details." He lightly caressed her collarbone.

"But we're leaving tonight," Zoe pointed out.

"That's for one of my assistants to worry about."

"But—"

He curled his fingers along the edge of her sheet and pulled it from her loose grasp. It fell to the floor and he kicked it to the side. "There are many other things on your to-do list before we leave," he said as his gaze roamed her body. "Returning to bed is at the top of that list."

Nadir curled his arms around her waist and lifted her up. Zoe didn't protest. She wrapped her legs around his waist and speared her hands in his hair before she kissed him.

As he rushed blindly for the bed Nadir knew relocating the honeymoon had nothing to do with the tribe's opinion. He wanted Zoe with him for a little longer. And it wasn't just because of the incredible sex. At this rate he would gain her complete trust and loyalty before the honeymoon ended.

The black sedan purred to a stop a few feet away from a sleek private jet. Zoe closed her eyes and ordered herself to remain calm. She had to play it cool or she would raise suspicion. There was no excuse to mess up when she was so close to escaping.

She opened her eyes and reached for Nadir's hand as he helped her out of the car. She moved with precision, although her limbs were weak with nerves. She stood on the tarmac at Omaira International airport and looked around.

She couldn't believe she was just a few steps away from leaving Jazaar. Forever. There had been times when she hadn't thought this moment would come, but now after all these years she was about to leave. In style, she thought with wicked amusement as she glanced at the red carpet rolled out for them.

She should feel relieved. Unencumbered. Zoe slowly exhaled as she walked onto the carpet. She wasn't sure exactly what she was feeling. Excited. Overwhelmed. Scared.

The desert wind pulled at her hair and her designer dress. The high heels she wore felt strange. Gone were the threadbare hand-me-downs and ill-fitting sandals. She was about to cast off that part of her life and go after her dreams.

She wrapped her hand around the stair railing and made her way to the door of the private plane. *Just a couple more steps...* Her chest was tight with apprehension. What if Nadir changed his mind at the last minute? What if there was a delay?

Even if the plane took off on time she wasn't exactly

home free. Singapore was far away from Houston, Texas. And she didn't have access to her new passport. Zoe worried her bottom lip. One of Nadir's many assistants had it for safekeeping.

She wasn't going to think about that right now. Today she was closer to her goal than she had been the day before. She was going to create a wonderful life and make something of herself. She had to remain focused and not get distracted by the sexual chemistry she shared with Nadir.

As she reached the plane's door Zoe greeted the flight attendant with a polite smile. She was about to cross the threshold when she froze. She felt a curious pull that made her turn around and take one last look at the deserts of Jazaar.

She stared in the direction of her old village. It was miles away, and she couldn't see it, but she had the awful feeling that the place would remain a part of her. Would this new world, this new life, be any better than the one she was leaving behind?

"It's beautiful, isn't it?" Nadir said at her side. She glanced up and saw him looking at the majestic sand dunes. "I've been all over the world and nothing compares."

Zoe pressed her lips together. She knew better than to argue, but it made her wonder how she could have anything in common with Nadir. How could she have a kinship with someone who adored her prison? He might have good memories and be tethered to his desert kingdom, but she wanted to forget everything that had happened to her here. Pretend that this place had never existed.

She turned abruptly and entered the plane. She halted and stared at the sleek lines and modern decor. It was like walking into a luxury home. The cream leather seats promised the ultimate comfort and the soft green sofas beckoned for travelers to kick back with a drink and chat. A door at the rear offered a glimpse of an elegant dining room and a curving staircase that led to another floor. She'd never seen anything like this and was tempted to explore.

It was also a surprise to see men in business suits typing away on their laptop computers and speaking quietly on their cell phones.

"These are a few of my employees working on the negotiations," Nadir said after he'd greeted the flight attendant. "I'll introduce you once we are in flight."

Zoe gave a nod and went for a leather chair at the back of the room. Maybe it was a habit to find the quietest, farthest corner, but she did not want to be in the way of the hardworking team. She buckled up and grabbed her e-reader from her bag.

As she turned on the device, eager to delve into a new story, she felt compelled to look out the window. She didn't move as the sun began to set. She watched the vibrant colors streak across the sky as Nadir sat down next to her.

"Why are you sitting all the way back here?" he asked.

"I didn't want to intrude on your business." She felt the plane begin to move and glanced over at Nadir as he buckled his seat belt. "I don't need to be entertained. I have my e-reader."

The plane picked up speed. This was it. She was leaving Jazaar. Her heart started to beat hard against her chest. She curled her hands around her seat belt.

"You don't like flying?" Nadir reached for her hand and laced his fingers with hers.

It wasn't that. After six years of planning and praying, she was out of Jazaar. It was too good to be true. As the plane lifted into the air Zoe closed her eyes and emotion clawed her throat. She was free. She gripped Nadir's hand. She was finally free.

She fought for composure. She didn't want Nadir to see how important this flight was for her. She slowly opened her eyes and glanced out the window. The tightness in her chest loosened and she exhaled shakily. The sun glowed against the sand dunes.

"You keep glancing back," Nadir mused. "Are you already getting homesick?"

She'd been homesick for six years, the longing so strong and thick that it almost suffocated her. "I don't have the same affection for Jazaar as you do," she said hoarsely as she removed her hand from his. "If I were a powerful sheikh I might feel homesick for the one place where I reign supreme."

"Your opinion may change now that you're a sheikha."

It was unlikely. A cage was a cage, no matter how gilded it might be. "I think I'd need to do a lot of traveling before I would miss Jazaar."

"You'll have to make the most of this trip." Nadir leaned his head back on the soft leather seat. "After our honeymoon, my plan is to delegate most of my traveling."

Her heart lurched. "Really? Why?"

"The initiatives I'm making for Jazaar's future are demanding more of my time and attention. I need to be here."

Zoe glanced back at the desert through the window as shock reverberated in her chest. She'd had no idea that he was ending his jet-setting ways. She had married him at the right time. If he planned to curtail his traveling this was her one chance to escape.

"You're surprised by my decision?" Nadir asked. "I don't understand why. My obligation is to Jazaar."

"Um…" She tried to keep her expression blank as she faced him. "You don't strike me as a stay-at-home kind of guy."

"Is that right?" His gaze ensnared hers and she saw the

amusement in his dark eyes. "What kind of man *do* you think I am?"

Zoe grimaced. She'd kind of walked right into that one. She wouldn't dare tell Nadir that she found him a man of sophistication and glamour. He was a sensual man, a sexy man who could easily seduce her.

He smiled and her heart skipped a beat. She couldn't quite look away from the breathtaking sight. It transformed him as the harsh features and deep grooves softened. She wished he would smile more often.

"Your eyes are very expressive," he said.

Her face burned bright. She wanted to squeeze her eyes shut but she refrained. "You have no idea what I'm thinking."

His smile slanted with knowing. "If we were alone," he said in a low, husky voice, "I would grant your wish and seduce you right now."

Her body jumped to attention as he made the husky promise. A warm ache twisted low in her belly. She needed to break the spell he had woven between them. She hectically looked around and saw one of Nadir's employees hovering nearby.

She dipped her head and stared at her e-reader, although she couldn't focus on the screen. "I believe you are needed up-front," she muttered under her breath.

"I believe I'm needed right here." He rubbed his thumb against her wrist. She knew he could feel her erratic pulse.

Zoe cleared her throat. "Anticipation makes it sweeter. Haven't you heard?"

"It doesn't make *you* sweeter," Nadir murmured, his thumb drawing circles on the inside of her wrist. "It makes you more demanding, more aggressive, even—"

She sharply turned her head and met his gaze. "If you don't know what to do with a strong woman in bed…"

"Oh, I know exactly what to do." He lifted her stiff hand and brushed his lips against her knuckles. "And you'll find out once we're alone in our hotel room."

Her body clenched as heat stung her skin.

He lowered her hand and moved away. "But now I have to attend to business." He released his seat belt. "Think of all the possibilities while I'm gone."

The pulsating energy evaporated the moment Nadir left. As she watched him approach his waiting employee Zoe wanted to sag against her seat. She pressed her hand against her flushed face, knowing she would spend the entire flight imagining what they would do once they arrived at their hotel.

What was she doing, teasing this man? Did she think the moment she was out of Jazaari rule she could regain her boldness? Nadir was a powerful man, a fearsome sheikh.

Not to mention a bold and audacious lover. Red-hot memories tumbled through her mind. The night before he had taken her countless times and—

Oh, my God. Zoe clutched the armrests and pitched forward as panic ripped through her. They hadn't been using protection. Not once.

Why hadn't she thought about this before? She had taught family planning to the women in her tribe. She knew better!

Zoe frantically worked out the dates in her sluggish mind. She worked them out again. It wasn't the right time of the month for her to become pregnant, but it was still a risk.

She turned to look out the window. Dread weighed heavily on her shoulders. She caught a last glimpse of the desert before her view was shrouded by the clouds.

She clapped her hand over her mouth as her stomach twisted cruelly. There was only one thing that could trap her in Jazaar. Having Nadir's baby.

CHAPTER NINE

SINGAPORE wasn't what she had expected, Zoe decided as she rode the hotel's private elevator with Nadir. She had imagined the scent of tropical flowers permeating thick, humid air. She had thought she would be greeted by a young, vibrant atmosphere and an explosion of color.

The elevator doors quietly slid open and revealed the dramatic entrance to the penthouse suite. The dark wood lattice walls flanked a wide window that provided a stunning view of a glittery skyline. An enormous round table sat in the middle of the room. In the center of the table was a slender glass vase with a deceptively simple arrangement of bright red orchids.

A crack of lightning forked through the dark sky and illuminated the fierce tropical storm that had greeted her the moment she'd stepped out of the airplane. Zoe flinched as a deafening clap of thunder boomed over their heads. Nadir placed a firm hand on her spine and escorted her out of the elevator.

She was very aware that she didn't jump when Nadir touched her. Was he aware of the significance? Did he realize that after years of dodging, evading and instinctively protecting her back, she now accepted his casual touch with just a moment's hesitation?

They were met by the penthouse butler, a formally

dressed older man. He bowed low with a respectful greeting and guided them into an opulent drawing room.

A butler? Zoe bit her bottom lip as she followed, acutely
aware of Nadir's hand resting possessively on her hip. She
didn't know penthouse suites had a servant on-call. That
was going to make it more difficult to slip away unnoticed.

Another jagged bolt of lightning sliced through the sky
and Zoe braced herself for the thunder. The immediate
rumble sounded ominous, and she instinctively curled
against Nadir's side.

"The storm will pass soon," he murmured in her ear as
he tightened his hold. "They don't last very long."

Zoe wasn't so sure about that. The storm howled in
growing fury and the rain lashed against the windows,
but she wasn't going to tremble or slink into a corner. She
had learned never to show her vulnerabilities in front of
anyone and she wasn't going to start now. She was embarrassed that Nadir noticed her moment of cowardice and
grateful that he didn't tease her.

As the butler offered tea, Zoe was pleased that her
hands were steady when she took the fragile china cup.
She stepped away from Nadir's hold and sat on a sleek
black sofa.

She didn't know what was wrong with her. She had to
snap out of it. She had dealt with plenty of thunderstorms
when she was growing up in Texas, but it had been a while
since she'd seen one.

Zoe hoped she hadn't lost her steely nerve along with
everything else. She needed it now more than ever if she
was going to grab her chance for freedom.

Once the butler departed lightning flashed again, cast-
ing the room with an eerie glow. Zoe cautiously placed
her teacup on a low table before the thunder rumbled.

Her spine straightened as she felt the sizzling tension in the room.

She was alone with Nadir. She couldn't help but glance in his direction. He watched her with intensity. The naked desire in his eyes made her shiver with anticipation.

Zoe bit her lip and dragged her gaze away. She would have to ward him off. No way could she risk a pregnancy—not when she was inching closer to her goal.

She didn't want to avoid Nadir. She was eager for his company…for his attention. It was definitely a sign that she needed to move on before she got in too deep with him.

"They are waiting for me at the office," Nadir said with a hint of regret.

"I'll find something to occupy my time," Zoe promised briskly as she rose from her seat. She wanted him to leave, but at the same time she wanted him to stay.

"No need." Nadir flicked his sleeve and looked at his watch. "Your assistant will be here in a few moments to go over your itinerary."

"My assistant?" Why did she need an assistant? Or was that code for babysitter? "Hold on. Did you say I have an itinerary?"

"Yes." Nadir set down his drink. "Rehana will take you shopping, to the spa and sightseeing."

She was right. The assistant was really a nanny, a minder. That would ruin all her plans. She had to think fast and get rid of the assistant without making Nadir suspicious.

Zoe slowly approached him. "That's very thoughtful of you, but I—"

"And your Arabic tutor will arrive later this afternoon."

She stumbled to a halt and stared at him. "You arranged lessons for me?"

"I told you I would." He frowned. "Why are you surprised?"

"I…" She had prepared herself for disappointment, assuming he wouldn't remember his promise. "Most of the men in my family are against educating women."

Nadir's eyebrow arched. "And you thought I shared the same views as your uncle?"

"No! No, of course not." She had been trying so hard not to say that, but Nadir had clearly read her mind. "The tutor is a wonderful surprise. Thank you."

Zoe brushed her lips against his cheek. She felt the muscle bunch in his jaw. Tension radiated from him. She knew Nadir was exerting his willpower and holding back. The gesture of thanks was a mistake. She knew better. One kiss was all it took for them to wind up in bed.

"I should go," he said gruffly, his gaze on her mouth. He swallowed hard. "If you need anything let the butler know. He will always be here."

At this rate she'd have an entire entourage with her when she tried to leave. "Nadir, I appreciate everything you've done for me, but it's not necessary. I'm looking forward to exploring on my own."

Nadir's eyes narrowed. "You will not go out alone."

Zoe folded her hands and fought to control her temper. Why must he say it like that? She was smart and capable. "English is spoken here," she reminded him. "I can navigate."

Nadir shook his head. "Your guide and a driver will be with you at all times."

Zoe squeezed her fingers together. She kept perfectly still as her mind raced. How was she going to look for the American embassy or hop on a plane to Texas when everyone was keeping an eye on her?

She reached out and cupped her hand against his angular jaw. She enjoyed seeing his eyes darken. She knew this was the last time she would have a chance to touch him. Once he left the suite she would disappear from his life.

"You don't have to feel guilty about leaving me alone on our honeymoon," she said earnestly. "I know how to take care of myself. I'm used to it."

"And your family were quite used to the trouble you caused when you were by yourself," Nadir murmured. He turned his head and placed a kiss in the center of her palm.

Another bolt of lightning ricocheted across the dawn sky. Zoe's breath hitched in her throat as she watched the brilliant light flash across the dramatic features of Nadir's face. He looked rough and dangerous. Sexy.

She felt her skin flush and tighten. Her hand tingled under his mouth. She wanted more of this. More of *him*.

Maybe it wasn't smart to make a run for it within minutes of arriving in Singapore. She held his gaze as the electric tension shimmered between them. Perhaps she should get familiar with Singapore and create a strategy. She could leave any time within the next few days.

Nadir reached for his cell phone and punched a button. "Rehana? Change of plans. You won't be needed today," he said as he pressed his lips against the inside of Zoe's wrist. "Let them know I won't make it to the office for a couple more hours."

"You're not going to the office?" Zoe asked as she watched him turn off his phone. "I thought you were needed for intense negotiations. It's the whole reason we're in Singapore."

He tossed the phone on the table. "I'm delegating because I have more important things to do."

She frowned. "Such as?"

A smile tugged at the corner of his mouth. "Spending the morning with my wife."

Zoe slowly blinked. That was the last thing she'd expected him to say. He wanted to be with her, too. A warm, tingly feeling washed over her. "You don't need to," she said softly.

"I want to." His dark eyes sparkled. "And you want me to as well."

He thought this was all to get more attention from him? What arrogance! If only he knew she was trying to get some time alone. "I didn't say that."

"You didn't have to," Nadir said. He slid his hand over hers and laced their fingers.

And at that moment she wanted to be with him. Spend time together. She wanted to act like newlyweds, even if it was pretend. This was an arranged marriage, not a love match.

"What if I ask you to cancel my itinerary?" she asked hopefully.

"I will for the morning," he compromised as he pressed his mouth against her temple. "But you *will* meet your tutor."

Zoe made a face. "This is supposed to be my honeymoon, not a special brand of torture. It took me forever to learn how to speak Arabic."

"You need to learn how to read it," Nadir said. He pressed another kiss against her cheek. "How else are you going to read bedtime stories to our babies?"

"Babies?" Her heart lurched. Where had *that* idea come from?

"Yes, babies," Nadir said smoothly, although he seemed as surprised as she was by his comment. "I expect more than one."

Of course he would. He was the heir to the throne. She should have thought about this! "We have never spoken about having children." Now was the time to tell him she wasn't ready for a baby.

"What is there to talk about?" he murmured.

"Plenty." Zoe closed her eyes, her mind whirling, as he caught her earlobe between his teeth. She shivered as the hot sensation sparked just under her skin. She wanted to forget everything and indulge in the pleasure.

She knew what she couldn't say. That the only time she would become pregnant was when she was in a solid and loving relationship. That she needed to feel safe and free before she brought a child into the world.

"I need an heir," Nadir said softly. "Jazaar is already on baby watch. There's hope that we will have a baby boy nine months from now."

"Jazaar can wait."

"But can I? I like the idea of you carrying my baby." She heard the male satisfaction in his husky voice.

Of course he would, Zoe decided. She shouldn't read anything in what he said. A pregnant sheikha was a sign of the Sheikh's strength and virility. It had nothing to do with how he felt about her.

"You want me to have your baby? *Me?*" She didn't fit any requirement for a good Jazaari bride. Why would he think she could make a good Jazaari mother?

"You are the Sheikha. My only wife. Who else can give me a legitimate heir?"

Ah, *that* was how she met the qualifications. Zoe struggled to collect her thoughts. "Nadir, I'm not ready to have children."

He went still and slowly lifted his head. "What are you saying?"

"I think we should use birth control," she said carefully, but she couldn't bring herself to meet his gaze. "I'll take care of everything. In fact I'll meet with a doctor today."

There was a long pause and Nadir took a step back. "You don't want my baby?"

She winced. "I—I didn't say that. I'm saying—"

"That you don't want my baby right now?" he said in a low, restrained tone.

She was making this worse. Zoe knew she had to explain, but she was hesitant to bring up her dreams. She had never talked about her goals much because the only way she could protect them from her family was to keep them secret.

Nadir was different from anyone she had met in Jazaar. If he understood why those goals were important to her he wouldn't get in her way. He might actually show her support.

"You may not know this, but I have a few goals," she said, looking down at the ground as her pulse quickened. "I want to accomplish some things before I have a family."

"What are your goals?"

She dared a glance in Nadir's direction. He seemed genuinely interested. No, it was more than that, Zoe realized as the hope swelled in her chest. He was pleased that she was sharing something about herself.

She nervously swiped her tongue across her bottom lip. "I want to complete my education."

"I also want that for you," he said with a shrug. "That's not a problem. Your Arabic tutor is just the beginning."

"I want more than a basic education," Zoe explained, her words coming out in an excited rush. "I want to become a doctor."

"A doctor?" Nadir repeated dully. What had he started? He had no idea why he had mentioned babies earlier. Though he was warming up to the idea of Zoe being pregnant with his child, especially after she'd displayed courage and loyalty at their last wedding ceremony.

And a moment ago he had been pleased that she was finally opening up to him. It was a sign of her trust in him. Now he had to deny her that dream.

"Honestly, I don't know if I have what it takes to become a doctor," she said. Her face was aglow with enthusiasm as she gestured with her hands to emphasize her point. "But I want to continue the work of my parents."

His gut twisted. He'd had no idea she had ambitious plans for her future. Plans that interfered with her new role.

"No."

His voice was soft but it affected Zoe like the lash of a whip.

Her eyes widened and her hands froze in midair. "Did you just say no?"

"Having a career outside the palace is not practical. As much as I want to modernize Jazaar, they would not understand a working sheikha."

"They'll get used to it," she promised.

Nadir shook his head. "My detractors already think I am too Western. Having an American wife with career ambitions would give them too much ammunition."

Zoe dropped her hands to her sides. "I see. You need to show that you have tamed your American bride."

He wouldn't have put it that bluntly, but it was the truth. He needed to show every tribal lord that he embraced their culture while dragging them into this century. "I need a sheikha who will honor tradition," he said. "A woman who symbolizes all of Jazaar's values."

"Beauty, refinement and obedience." She spat out the words with disgust. "Have you considered that becoming a doctor would *enhance* my role as sheikha?"

"No. The sheikha's role is to support her husband. Nothing else can take priority."

He saw the impotent anger in Zoe's eyes. The determined set of her jaw. She was willing to fight for her dreams even if it meant going against him. It was clear that she saw him as the enemy.

Nadir swallowed a sigh. She would never see that he was protecting her, not destroying her. The draconian palace officials would fight her every step of the way, and they wouldn't stop there. The officials had outdated views about women. They would quash her spirit so she would remain obedient.

It would be best for her if she didn't cling to her dreams. She needed to pick her battles carefully.

He wondered why Zoe's family hadn't warned her about the sacrifices she would have to make to become Sheikha. They probably didn't care. They were only concerned about the bridal price and their connection to the royal family.

Zoe never should have married him. She didn't fit any of the requirements to be a royal bride. Not only had she given up her lover to be at his side, but she had future ambitions that she was not allowed to pursue. And she wasn't the type to surrender her dreams. He was going to have a fight on his hands.

Nadir crossed his arms and braced his legs. "Zoe, there are some things you can't do because you're the Sheikha. The logistics and security measures would be impossible. A doctor's duties would challenge a sheikha's rules of conduct. A career is just not feasible. You can be a patron or president of a medical charity, but you can't work as a doctor."

Zoe's eyes narrowed and her lush mouth drew into a firm line. "Taking care of the women in my tribe was the only thing that got me through the days."

"And now you have a new tribe and a new role."

She closed her eyes and exhaled sharply. "This is unfair. I never wanted to be a princess or a sheikha. I've always wanted to be a doctor."

"You have already made your choice, Zoe."

"I didn't make the choice," she said bitterly. "The choice was made for me."

"I'm not going to change my mind," Nadir warned her, his voice soft and lethal. "This conversation is over."

She clenched her hands and thrust out her chin. She wasn't going to let him see her crushing disappointment. It was her only protection. This was why she'd kept her dreams a secret.

Why had she even thought the Sheikh would be an ally? Because of his progressive ideas? Or had she mistaken his amazing lovemaking skills for actual caring? Nadir could pretend to be a thoughtful husband, but he made it very clear that he saw her as an interchangeable accessory.

She wanted to fight harder. Fight dirty. But she would run the risk of revealing too much, and Nadir could use that against her. Zoe slowly unclenched her fists and fought for composure. Why bother fighting? She was going to leave him and go back to Texas. He could make plans for her. She wouldn't be here to follow through.

"Fine," she bit out. She couldn't look at him, knowing her eyes flashed with defiance. She felt his surprise and suspicion at her quick capitulation. "But I'm still going to a doctor about birth control," she said as she turned on her heel and headed for the doorway.

"You still don't want my baby?" he drawled.

"Maybe I want the honeymoon to last a little longer," she said sarcastically over her shoulder.

"If that's what you want," Nadir said, "we won't try to have children until after our first wedding anniversary."

She whirled around. She was stunned that he'd agreed to one of her wishes. What was he up to? She studied his expression and he appeared sincere. "Do you really mean that?"

Nadir slowly approached her. "But you might already be pregnant."

Zoe shook her head. "It's the wrong time of the month for me, but I'll have the doctor verify that today."

"Good." He cupped her elbow. "And I meant what I said about the medical charities. You could do great work without being a doctor."

Zoe stared at his hand and gave a sharp nod. She didn't trust herself to speak. He thought he was being magnanimous. He didn't understand that what he was offering was a transfer from a small cage to a slighter bigger one.

She was not going to get the support she needed from Nadir. It didn't matter that she was becoming addicted to his touch or that she felt closer to him than anyone else. She had to leave him or she would lose everything again.

CHAPTER TEN

Zoe's polite smile was about to fall off as she said goodbye to her assistant and stepped into the penthouse the next afternoon. The moment she heard the elevator doors slide shut her shoulders sagged with relief.

"I swear, that woman is going to drive me crazy," she muttered under her breath. She heard footsteps and saw the butler approach. Would she ever get a moment to herself? All she needed was one minute to disappear. Just one minute. Was that too much to ask?

"Your Highness," the butler greeted her as he gave a bow and took her packages. "The Sheikh is in the drawing room."

That surprised her. Zoe glanced at her wristwatch, but she still had plenty of time to prepare for the charity gala they had to attend. Why was Nadir here? Perhaps her question should be what rule had she broken this time to warrant Nadir's early arrival?

She strode into the drawing room with her head held high. She knew she looked like a polished princess from head to toe, thanks to a day at the spa and salon. She had been on edge and impatient, waiting for a chance to run away, but that tenacious assistant had never allowed her a moment alone.

She halted when she saw Nadir stretched out on the

long sofa. His jacket had been discarded and his tie was askew. A whisky tumbler sat on the ornate carpet by the sofa. His eyes were closed.

Now, her mind screamed as she stared at him. *This is the minute you've been searching for. You will never see Nadir this unguarded again. Disappear!*

She'd rolled back on her heel, prepared to make a dash for the elevator, when she studied his face. He looked exhausted and pale. The lines in his face were etched deep. Was he ill?

She pressed her lips together as she was swamped by indecision. Should she stay or should she go? She clenched her fists and sighed. She'd better not regret this choice, but if Nadir was unwell she needed to help him. She could find a different time to disappear. Hopefully.

"Is there something that you want?" Nadir asked. He didn't move and he kept his eyes closed.

Zoe dipped her head. She should have known he'd been aware of her the moment she'd stepped into the room. Nothing got past him.

She slowly walked to the sofa, finding it strange to look down at him. "Are you feeling all right?" she asked. She placed a hand on his forehead. His skin was cool to the touch.

He caught her wrist in his firm grasp without opening his eyes. It was only then that she realized this was the first time in their marriage that she had reached out and touched him outside their bed. Zoe hoped Nadir didn't read anything into that gesture. No, she decided. It would be beneath his notice.

"I'm fine," he said. "I'm thinking about the next move in my negotiation strategy."

"If you say so, but in Texas we call this a nap." She

gave a tug, but he didn't release her. "I'm going to get ready for the gala."

"I'm at stalemate," he confessed wearily. "I can't get them to accept my terms. And do you know why?"

She looked around the room. Was he talking to *her*? A Jazaari man didn't discuss business with a woman. Everyone knew that. "Uh…no…?" she said tentatively as she checked for signs of delirium.

"They think that I hold the same antiquated beliefs as the Sultan. No one is willing to invest in Jazaar because they think nothing will change when I rule." His eyes opened suddenly and his gaze held hers. "Do you think I'm a modern man?"

She felt his strong fingers around her wrist. She could lie, but he genuinely wanted her answer. "No."

Nadir's eyes narrowed. "No?"

Zoe gave another tug but couldn't break free. Maybe she should have lied. "I think you are more forward-thinking than the men in Jazaar. But compared to the men in other countries, no, you aren't modern."

He stared at her and heavy silence pulsed in the room. He slowly uncurled his fingers from her wrist. "Thank you for your honesty," he said coldly.

She drew her hand away from him. "I didn't mean to insult you."

"You didn't." He sat up and rested his elbows on his legs.

She had a feeling that she had offended him. Zoe sat down on the edge of the coffee table. "What company are you negotiating with? How modern are they?"

"They are a telecommunications company. My goal is for everyone in Jazaar to have access."

"Really?" She leaned back in surprise. Nadir was more aware of his countrymen's needs than she had first realized. His goal would bring a positive impact to the remote areas, and providing instant information to everyone would also reshape the tribal hierarchy. Zoe smiled at the possibilities. "So, what's the problem?"

Nadir ran his hands through his dark, thick hair. "The company is owned by a socially conscious widow."

"Ah." And Jazaar was not known for its women's rights. "Are you negotiating directly with the widow?"

"No," he said tightly, and Zoe knew it was a blow to his pride that he was dealing with an underling. "But she is very involved with the negotiations."

How could Nadir prove his modern approach? Whatever he said or did would be influenced by their preconceived ideas. Unless…

"Will she be at the charity ball?"

Nadir looked at Zoe with growing suspicion. "Yes, her company is sponsoring it."

Zoe began to rub her hands together as she formed a plan. "Then it's time to reveal your secret weapon."

Nadir tilted his head as if he was bracing himself for bad news. "And that would be…?"

Zoe spread her arms out wide. "Me."

He stared at her with disbelief. "You?"

"Yes, me. Your thoroughly modern American bride." She shimmied her shoulders. "Come on—you know I would knock all their preconceived notions on their asses."

He groaned and covered his eyes with his hands. "Zoe, you are not ready to represent Jazaar."

"I may not represent Jazaar to the people of Jazaar, but what about representing the new and improved Jazaar to other countries?"

Nadir slowly leaned back and studied her intently. He was seriously considering what she had said. Zoe was glad she was looking her finest.

She saw his gaze harden. "What are you really up to?" he asked.

She frowned and lowered her arms. "Nothing."

He slowly shook his head, as if that couldn't possibly be the right answer. "Why do you suddenly want to help me?"

Good question. This guy was keeping her from what she wanted most. He had too much power over her life and her future. It would be better to sabotage him, but she didn't want to. "Maybe I'm trying to do something nice."

Nadir's eyebrows went up.

She scowled at him. "It's been known to happen."

"I'm sure it has, but you're unpredictable." He shook his finger at her. "You could start an international incident without trying."

She folded her arms. "Do you want my help or not?"

"Okay, Zoe, I would like you to represent Jazaar." He reluctantly accepted her help. "But if you go too far…"

"Trust me, Nadir." She rose to her feet. "By the end of the night you are going to see me in a whole new light."

Nadir heard the orchestra play a final note with a flourish as they left the charity gala. He held Zoe's hand firmly while he led her down the steps to the waiting limousine.

"I look forward to meeting you tomorrow," he said to the vice-president of the telecommunications company. He felt triumph rolling through Zoe and gently squeezed her hand in warning.

"I'm sure we can negotiate terms that will satisfy all parties," Mr. Lee said. "Also, Mrs. Tan invites you and your wife to her home later this week to celebrate the deal."

"We would be honored," Zoe replied.

Nadir helped her into the limousine, fighting the urge to bolt before she caught him by surprise again. He said goodbye to Mr. Lee and unhurriedly got into the limo himself. As the car pulled away from the curb he slowly exhaled. He had never considered galas exciting, but tonight had been a rollercoaster thanks to his wife.

"I think that went well," Zoe said, resting her head against the leather seat. "I didn't want to leave."

"Why? Did you want one more victory lap around the ballroom?"

She laughed. It was unbridled and earthy. Very unprincess-like. The Sheikha didn't know protocol or diplomacy, but it didn't matter. Zoe had proved she was a brazen and modern woman. A new breed of royalty.

"I told you I was your secret weapon. You didn't believe me, did you? But you let me go after it because you had nothing to lose."

It was true. He hadn't had high hopes of getting back to the negotiating table, but Zoe knew how to present them as a modern couple. Most of the time. "I should have brought a muzzle for you," he said on a low growl.

Zoe laughed again. "It would have clashed with my gown."

His gaze traveled down the lilac gown. It was a modest design but the delicate fabric hugged her body. She'd been the sexiest woman at the event, overshadowing those who wore barely-there dresses.

He shook his head and tore his gaze from her body. He would not get distracted. "You just couldn't help yourself, could you?"

Zoe's smile grew wide. "I'm sorry."

No, she wasn't. She had planned the surprise attack to test her power and his patience. It was strange he wasn't angry about it. He only wished he had had a little more warning. "I'm creating a domestic violence program?" he said. "Since when?"

"It kind of slipped out when I spoke to Mrs. Tan," she

said with a shrug. "And it sounded really good so I just went with it."

"It was a very detailed lie. A twenty-four-hour crisis line? Group counseling? Emergency shelter? You came up with all that on the spot?"

"Those are some of the services my mother volunteered at back home. We could use them in the village," she explained. "I guess you could tell Mrs. Tan that you can't push your program through the bureaucracy."

"I don't think so." It was a good idea, and he wished Zoe had had those resources when she'd needed them.

"What are you going to do?"

"Make it happen." Warmth spread through his chest when he saw Zoe's eyes light up. "It will be your project."

Her jaw dropped. "My project?"

"It's your lie," he reminded her as he held her hand. "Anyway, you know what the program needs."

"I don't know if that's a good idea. I might mess up."

"I doubt that."

She looked out the window. Nadir studied her, wondering why he'd never considered that Zoe would be an asset to him. She was fearless in telling him the truth and could become a powerful ally.

She had already created an opportunity that had been denied to him. She could recreate the image of Jazaar and improve business and diplomatic relations if he had her at his side.

But she was still a liability when they were in Jazaar. It would be safer for her if he hid her in the mountain palace, yet he was no longer considering that an option. Until he had to make a decision about her future he would show his modern sheikha to the world.

The music pulsed in synch with the lights and Zoe felt the primitive beat vibrating under the dance floor. The people around her swayed their arms and hips to the sensual beat. Zoe curled her arms over Nadir's shoulders and moved even closer to him. She was rewarded by the gleam of his eyes.

A sense of joy and promise flooded her body. The week in Singapore had been the happiest she had known in a long time. Even the Arabic tutorials hadn't dimmed her spirits. She had dreaded the lessons, remembering the struggle she had had learning the language when she'd first arrived in Jazaar. But this time it wasn't as frustrating or as painful because no one was expecting immediate results. She felt as if her world was expanding each day, each hour.

She had shed the caftans and robes of Jazaar for younger, brighter clothes. Clothes that reflected who she was, not who people wanted her to be. During the week she had met interesting people and explored Singapore. Yet her favorite moments had been the ones she'd shared alone with Nadir.

She hadn't expected someone as sophisticated as Nadir to accompany her to all the tourist attractions. She knew he was extremely busy, but all his attention was on her when they were together. Whether it was sharing a kiss on the cable car ride to Sentosa Island, or discovering Singapore's glittering nightlife, Nadir seemed more fascinated by her than his surroundings.

But it was time to go, Zoe thought with a hint of sadness. Nadir's business negotiations were finalized. She had an escape plan ready. She shivered as she thought about the risky maneuver. She had to go now if she didn't want to be carted back to Jazaar.

She had to leave if she wanted to give her dreams a chance, but she was strangely reluctant to go.

"Thank you for bringing me to this nightclub, Nadir.

I've never been to one." Even if she had been invited to dance at a wedding or festival she wouldn't have participated. She hadn't felt like dancing until now.

"Your wish is my command," he murmured in her ear.

If only. "It's going to be hard leaving Singapore." *Hard to leave him.* "I've had the time of my life."

Nadir raised his head and looked into her eyes. "You're not feeling homesick for Jazaar?"

She controlled her expression in case he saw her true feelings about Jazaar. "No, not at all."

Anticipation flickered in Nadir's dark eyes. "Then you will accompany me to Athens."

"Athens? As in Greece?" The cautious excitement hummed inside her. "Seriously?"

"I have some business there I need to attend to." Nadir's hands slid sensuously down the length of her spine and rested low on her hips. "I'm not sure how long it will take me."

"I would love to go," she said. "Did you know that Greece is the birthplace of western medicine?"

"Zoe…"

The soft warning in his voice punctured her enthusiasm. She knew better than to discuss that forbidden topic with him. She drew back until they were barely touching. "Sorry." She forced the word from her throat. "When do we go?"

Nadir gathered her close until she felt his strong heartbeat against her chest. "Tomorrow."

She wasn't sure if Greece was closer or farther away from America. It would be better to execute her plan tonight. But she wanted to be with Nadir. She wanted to pretend just a little longer.

He must have seen the need in her eyes. She felt the air around them spark as his harsh features darkened. Zoe's breath hitched in her throat as her skin tingled with anticipation.

"Let's go back to the hotel," he said abruptly, capturing her hand in his and leading her off the dance floor.

She stared at their joined hands as she followed him. His dark hand was large as it engulfed hers. She felt safe. Wanted. No longer alone.

It wasn't real, Zoe reminded herself. It felt incredibly genuine, but she was falling under the spell of a honeymoon. She should leave now, before she could no longer tell the difference between fantasy and reality. She should escape now in case she didn't get another chance.

She enjoyed being with Nadir. She had been so lonely before she met him, and she would be alone again once she left. She wanted to make the most of this moment. But when was the right time to leave?

Zoe continued to stare at her hand twined with Nadir's. She felt his urgency and her legs wobbled. Her gaze fastened on the deep brown and festive henna design that still decorated her hand. It reminded her of the young brides from the tribe.

Those brides never went on a trip for a honeymoon. It simply wasn't part of tradition. Instead the brides were treated like princesses, doing no housework or cooking until the henna wore off.

Zoe knew her decision was made when she focused on the floral design at the base of her thumb. In a week or two her honeymoon would be over. Once the henna faded, that would be her sign to walk away from Nadir and start her new life.

CHAPTER ELEVEN

"ARE you sure you want to know?" Zoe asked hesitantly.

Nadir's curious expression didn't change. "I asked, didn't I?"

She wondered why he'd chosen this moment to ask. They were curled up together in bed, naked and spent. She was lying on her stomach and facing him, her hands tucked under a goosedown pillow. Nadir was sprawled on his back, his face close to hers.

She suddenly knew the answer to her question. Her stomach twisted as she fought off the sinking feeling. Nadir had asked because she had finally lowered her guard.

They'd been traveling throughout Europe for the past week and a half, acting like newlyweds. Nadir had successfully wooed her into gradually opening up to him. It had been a determined, aggressive campaign and she had fallen for it.

She should be furious at herself for believing in the fantasy, for sharing too much. But it was strange; she didn't regret it. Zoe had come to the startling realization that she had never felt as close to anyone as she felt to Nadir.

At some time during the honeymoon that had started in Jazaar and had now moved to London she had started to trust Nadir. Just a little. She wasn't going to repeat her mistake and discuss her dreams, and she knew better than to reveal all of her deepest, darkest secrets.

"You don't have to tell me," Nadir said softly, and turned his head to look at the ceiling.

She hadn't realized she had allowed the pause to stretch for so long. "Sorry, I was trying to decide which mistake was the worst," Zoe said lightly. "I have so many to choose from."

She never should have started this ritual of sharing something about themselves right before they fell asleep. It was one thing to share a favorite color or a childhood memory. It was another thing to expose your weaknesses, mistakes and fears. Especially to someone who had the power to use that information against you.

"My worst mistake…" Zoe suddenly felt jittery and cold washed over her skin. She looked away and took a steady breath. "My worst mistake was probably Musad Ali. He was the son of our neighbor."

She felt the mood shift in the luxurious bedroom. She didn't have to spell it out that Musad had been her lover. Nadir slowly turned to face her.

Maybe it was wrong to share this part of her past. It was risky, but she wanted Nadir to understand her.

She focused on his broad shoulders. She had never told anyone about Musad. It was her secret, her shame. Maybe it wasn't a good idea to tell Nadir. Their intimate relationship could change from this moment on.

"Musad was the wrong man to get close to," she admitted hoarsely. "He was the wrong man to trust." She'd used to think all men were untrustworthy. Now she wasn't so sure.

"How long did it last?"

She blinked when she heard his calm question. Her gaze flickered across his face. He showed no judgment or anger. Was that really how he felt, or was he holding back so she would reveal more?

"About six months," she answered tentatively. "He promised to marry me before he went to college in Chicago. But he always intended to leave me behind."

"If your uncle had discovered the affair…" Nadir murmured.

Zoe shivered at the thought. "It was stupid. Reckless."

He reached out and rubbed his hand along her bare arm. "You were in love."

She hadn't been in love with Musad, but she was ashamed to admit it. Love could make a careless action seem noble. She, however, had made one bad decision after another.

"I was trapped in my uncle's house. Terrified and miserable," she explained. "When I was with Musad I could forget for a while. Musad promised he would take me away from it all, and I was so desperate to believe him I didn't see that it was just a line to get me into bed."

"How did your cousin find out?"

"I'm not sure." When Fatimah had taunted her with the information, it had blindsided Zoe. "I wonder if she saw us together. At the end, Musad was taking a lot risks. So was I. I wanted to rebel."

Nadir frowned. "He exposed you to danger."

"I don't think that was his intention," Zoe said. She didn't think very highly of Musad, but she also didn't believe that he was calculated or cruel. "Musad was selfish, and he used me, but he would also have been punished if our relationship had been discovered."

"But you would have been punished more," Nadir pointed out, his eyes narrowing with anger. "And you had to get out of your uncle's house before Tareef found out. Marriage was your only way out."

"Yes." Out of her uncle's home. Out of Jazaar. Out of hell.

"You were even willing to marry The Beast."

Zoe made a face. "I hate that nickname of yours. You are not a beast."

"Are you sure about that?"

His dark voice sent a shiver down her spine. Was she sure about him? Could he hide a violent nature until it was too late for her? He was different from her uncle and the men in the tribe, but he was also more powerful and dangerous.

"Now it's your turn," she whispered. She remained still but she was tempted to curl up in a protective ball. "What was *your* biggest mistake?"

A long pause hung between them. Zoe wanted to cringe because she knew she had crossed a forbidden boundary. He could ask personal questions, but it was impertinent for her to do the same.

"Yusra," Nadir answered. "She was my biggest mistake."

Zoe was surprised that he had spoken Yusra's name. He never talked about that night or the scandal that had tarnished his reputation. "Why?" she dared to ask.

"I should have exerted more self-control."

Zoe froze as her heart stopped. Her skin prickled with warning. What was he saying? That he deserved the nickname? That he had the potential to be wild and untamed as a beast?

Nadir suddenly rolled on top of her. Her heart beat hard against her ribs as she felt his erection against her skin. Should she be afraid of her husband?

"I will never allow my emotions get the better of me again," he promised hoarsely.

He wrapped his hands around her wrists and held her

arms above her head. He lowered his head and claimed her mouth with his. Her pulse skipped wildly as she responded to his determined touch.

When he broke the kiss, she stared into his dark eyes. She didn't speak but she wanted to shatter this moment. She saw the desire in Nadir's eyes, but she saw something else. Something dark and unreachable.

Whatever had happened on his wedding night with Yusra, he wouldn't tell her. He saw no need to explain his past actions or his cryptic words.

What was wrong with her? She should fight him off and escape. She should be afraid of him. Instead she lay underneath him, naked and vulnerable. Wildly excited and drawn to his darkness.

He kissed, licked and nibbled down the length of her body. The sound of her gasps and his murmurs of appreciation echoed in the room. She dug her fingers into his shoulders when he worshipped her breasts with his hands and mouth. She twisted the bedsheets in her fists as he darted his tongue into her navel.

Zoe bucked her hips as Nadir dipped his head between her legs. A shower of sparks tingled under her skin as he pleasured her with his mouth. Ribbons of desire danced through her blood. She tangled her fingers in his hair as need flashed hot. A moan was torn from her throat as she climaxed.

Pleasure still rippled through her as Nadir hooked her trembling legs around his lean hips. He surged into her, groaning as her body eagerly welcomed him. His powerful thrusts quickly became uneven and wild. Zoe clung to him, her legs wrapped tightly around him, as another climax tore through her.

She heard his harsh cry as he found his release. He slumped against her, his body slick with sweat. Her arms and legs felt weak, but she held him close, unwilling to let this moment go.

He rolled onto his back and she watched his chest rise and fall with each breath. Their arms were touching, his hand covering hers, but it wasn't enough for her. She must trust him on some level if she needed to be in his arms.

But if she asked it would show too much of how she felt. Zoe nervously curled against him and shivered. "It's freezing."

Nadir's chuckle sounded drowsy and he gathered her against his solid chest. "Hardly. September in London is glorious. You are simply used to the desert."

"You're probably right." She didn't like the idea that she was more comfortable in the desert than in a cosmopolitan city.

"Admit it," he said sleepily as his arms wrapped around her, "you miss Jazaar."

Zoe wanted to scoff at the suggestion when a memory assailed her. She remembered the quiet hush and the tantalizing spices. She had enjoyed looking out into the desert and watching the sun dip below the sand dunes. She had learned to appreciate the natural and harsh beauty of the arid region. "I miss some things." *But not deeply enough to go back.* "Like the heat."

Nadir's eyes gradually closed. "Then you will be happy to know that we will be somewhere warm this time tomorrow."

She went on the alert and her heart skipped a beat. Was he already planning to return to Jazaar? "Where are we going?" she asked cautiously.

"Mexico City."

Zoe's eyes widened. "Mexico...?" she said in a whispery breath. Mexico shared a border with Texas. She would be incredibly close to home.

"But until then I'm prepared to keep you warm." His words were slurred with sleep.

"That sounds like a good plan," she said. She cupped her hand against his cheek and stroked the dark stubble.

Zoe noticed that her henna had almost disappeared. Only a few stubborn swirls remained. It still counted, she decided, as she tilted her head to kiss Nadir. Her honeymoon would officially end in Mexico.

The decision should have filled her with hope and determination. Instead it made her want to make the most of the honeymoon before she walked away from her husband forever.

CHAPTER TWELVE

NADIR gratefully stepped into the hotel lobby and found the hushed surroundings were a peaceful oasis from the dynamic city. The soft cream sofas and the warm brown walls reminded him of the desert. Even the peasant art framed in gold made him think of Jazaar. He was working hard and traveling now so that afterward he could return home for good and take care of his country.

The meetings with his Mexico City office were becoming more difficult. As he walked past the elegant front desk Nadir admitted that it didn't help that he had been distracted. He had left Zoe, warm and willing, in their bed. The sex they had shared that morning had been nothing short of mind-blowing.

It had not been his best idea to mix his honeymoon with business trips. He'd thought he could get his fill of Zoe before he ensconced her in his mountain palace. Instead he had become insatiable for his wife. He couldn't imagine being away from her for more than a day.

Worse, he was starting to rely on her. On more than one occasion he had sought her opinion or her point of view. She was very knowledgeable, and provided him with a look into tribal life he could not get from any of his advisors.

Anticipation twanged in his blood as he headed for the elevators. When he saw the hotel manager hurrying to greet him he wanted to growl with frustration. He didn't want any more delays in returning to Zoe.

Nadir frowned. When had his every waking moment started to revolve around her? He didn't just want to bed her. He wanted to be with her. Spend every waking minute together. Shock reverberated through him. This was more than desire and lust. Was he falling for his arranged bride?

As he wrestled with that inconvenient thought, the hotel manager intercepted his path to the elevators. "Your Highness, I hope your stay has been pleasant," the man said with a slight bow. "I understand you are leaving us tomorrow?"

"Yes, we enjoyed our stay here, Señor Lopez."

"We are very fortunate that you have chosen our hotel." His smile suddenly brightened. "And may I say that your wife is an amazing woman?"

"Yes, she is." Zoe was a fighter, with survival instincts. She had the heart of warrior, the mind of a scientist, and the beauty of a goddess. He was proud to have her as his wife.

"So beautiful," Señor Lopez waved his hand to emphasize his point. "So brilliant, so curious."

Nadir went still. "Curious?"

The hotel manager bobbed his head. "Yes, she has taken great interest in the public health conference here at the hotel. The Sheikha has attended a few panels after meeting with the guest of honor. She fits right in."

Dark frustration spun inside him. Nadir struggled to keep a mildly interested expression. "Is that right?"

"She has quite a few ideas about maternal health. The debates can get…intense."

"I can imagine." He had forbidden her from medicine. He had trusted her. "The Sheikha never backs down."

Señor Lopez gave another small bow. "I hope the Sheikha enjoyed her stay?"

"I'm sure she did." He bade the hotel manager goodbye

and walked into the elevator on numb legs. Anger whipped through him as he gave a vicious swipe of his key card to activate the elevator.

It was time to go home. He had placed too much trust in Zoe. Given her too many liberties. Nadir knew he was beginning to sound like his father, but he didn't care. He had made those rules to help her assimilate into royal life and she had ignored them.

He'd managed to get his temper under control by the time he stepped into the penthouse suite. This time the soothing décor was invisible to him. All he noticed was that Zoe was not there to greet him. For some reason that made him angrier.

As the butler approached him with a wary smile, Nadir tersely asked for Zoe. He was informed that she was sunbathing. Nadir stalked to the private pool that was just off their bedroom.

His steps faltered when he saw her. She was lounging by the pool and reading an e-book. Her sunglasses were perched on her head and the modest blue swimsuit she wore skimmed her curves.

His stomach clenched as he silently watched her. Her dark hair was piled on top of her head. He didn't have to sink his fingers into it to know it would feel like warm silk. Her sun-kissed skin would be soft and fragrant. And her lips…Nadir's body hardened and his skin began to tingle. Zoe knew how to drive him wild with just her mouth.

She wasn't what he had expected in a wife. She was no Jazaari bride. She was sexy, opinionated and exciting. And disobedient. Nadir clenched his teeth. Extraordinarily disobedient.

When Nadir slid the door open, Zoe glanced up from her e-reader. The joy in her eyes and the wide, inviting smile surprised him. She was genuinely happy to see him.

Her smile dimmed when she caught his expression. "Bad day at the office?" she asked as she sat up.

"I understand you attended the public health conference?" he replied with icy calm.

As if a heavy curtain had fallen, Zoe's expression went blank. She looked down and turned off the e-book reader before setting it on the small table at her side. "I'm not sure who gave you that idea."

Nadir knew he was in for a battle. Zoe wasn't going to share any details. It was one more secret to hide from him.

"Should I call the assistant assigned to you and ask for details about your day?" He loosened his necktie with a vicious tug.

Zoe's mouth tightened. "No, there's no need for that. I attended a few events at the conference."

The vein in his forehead began to throb. He thrust his hands in his pockets. "After I told you to stay away from anything related to medicine?" he asked with lethal softness.

"The guest of honor invited me. He's a respected authority on newborn health!" Zoe insisted, jumping up from her lounge chair. "It would have been rude to decline."

"I'm sure you could have come up with an excuse."

Her jaw shifted to one side. "Why should I have made an excuse? I wanted to go. Those people understand me. I felt like I finally belonged somewhere."

"Don't disobey me again," he said in a fierce whisper.

Zoe went rigid, her body slightly shaking with tension. "It's not like I planned it!"

Her outburst surprised him. No one talked back when he gave a command. "I mean it, Zoe."

She didn't back down. She thrust her jaw out and her dark eyes glittered with defiance. "You are unreasonable.

There is nothing wrong with having opinions about medicine or having basic first aid skills."

"You won't need to use them."

"You don't know that. What if you collapse this very minute?" she asked, planting her hands on her hips. "Do you want me to stand back and hope someone else can help you?"

"Yes."

Zoe blinked. "Are you serious? You really wouldn't want my help?"

Nadir saw the hurt in her eyes. He wanted to erase the pain and tell her his decision had nothing to do with her abilities. But he needed to stay firm. Zoe needed to understand that she couldn't resurrect her old dreams. Those dreams had died the moment she married him. He hated the fact as much as she did, but it was time to move forward and not look back.

"My security detail is trained for any type of emergency," he explained. "If I found out you'd interfered with their jobs I would be furious."

"Well, I don't *have* a security detail."

"Yes, you do." Nadir frowned. How could she not know? Did she honestly think he wouldn't keep her safe?

She narrowed her eyes and tilted her head as she stared at him in confusion. "What are you talking about?"

"You have had a full security team following you since our wedding day. How else would I have found you when you wandered off into the bookstore in Omaira?"

She had a security detail. Her heart stopped as shock rippled through her body. There was a team of professionals who tracked her every move. She had had no idea.

She looked down and clasped her hands together in front of her. She couldn't let Nadir see the horror in her face. All this time she had been angry at herself for not taking any opportunity to escape. She had hesitated in Athens, procrastinated in Europe, and held back in Mexico. Yet had she tried to leave she would have failed spectacularly.

"Who? How many?" Zoe asked. She had no idea who was following her. She didn't recognize anyone as they traveled from one place to the next.

"That doesn't matter." Nadir dismissed the questions with a wave of his hand. "You are not playing doctor. I don't want to hear that you gave so much as a vitamin to someone."

She remained silent. How could she possibly make a promise like that? Didn't he know her at all?

"Zoe," he warned, "you need to learn how to obey."

She looked up at him from beneath her lashes. "Or what?"

Nadir's eyes darkened. "Don't push me."

"I know how *you* feel about the idea of me studying medicine. But do you know how I feel about it?" she asked bitterly. She lifted her head and met his gaze. "Do you know that I've always wanted to follow in my father's footsteps? That medicine fascinates me? Do you know? Do you care?"

Nadir slowly folded his arms. "I know that you have been fascinated by medicine since you were a candy striper when you were thirteen years old. You found the hospital atmosphere exciting, but what you really wanted to do was continue the work of your parents."

His answer astonished her. She hadn't thought he understood, but he knew exactly what drove her. And he would still keep her from her dream rather than support it.

She shouldn't be surprised, but she felt as if Nadir had betrayed her. She should have known better than to reveal what was important to her.

"I also suspect you're hiding a few medical thrillers on that e-reader."

She cast a guilty glance at her e-reader. "Oh." He was fine with her having a passing interest in medicine as long as she didn't use it.

"I'm protecting you from a battle you can't win."

"But you are keeping me away from something that I love."

"I know." Nadir thrust his fingers into his hair and exhaled sharply. "I will create a role for you in the medical community," he said slowly. "You can take a small part in our health ministry."

She drew her head back as her heart began to pump hard. Was Nadir truly bestowing an honor? She was almost afraid to believe there were no strings attached, no bait and switch. She hated being cynical, but it was her only armor. "There are no women in that ministry."

"There will be resistance," he said, and she could tell it was major understatement. "But it's nothing I can't handle. I know that the women's health system in our country is lacking, but I didn't understand how bad it was until I listened to your experiences."

"I'm not qualified," she was quick to point out. It was a prestigious position, but she was young, uneducated and female. "I don't think I would be very effective."

"You're the Sheikha. My wife. They will listen," he answered confidently.

"Thank you for the offer, Nadir. It's very generous." It wasn't her dream, but it was something. There was no guarantee that she could become a doctor, but with Nadir's proposition, she could change the way they practiced medicine in Jazaar. "I'll think about it."

Nadir reached out and cupped her face with his hands.

He tilted her face up and looked intently into her eyes. "That's the best offer you're going to get."

"I know." She was beginning to understand that. But she wanted to live her life on her own terms, and she didn't think she could do that if she was with him. She couldn't have everything and she needed to make a decision fast.

Nadir studied her expression for a moment. He sighed and dropped his hands. "You should get ready for dinner."

Zoe gave a nod and stepped away. The sun had dipped and it was getting cooler. "Where are we going?" she asked.

"On the jet."

She froze. They were leaving Mexico City earlier than planned. Zoe's gaze zoomed to her hands. The henna had disappeared days ago, but she hadn't made an attempt to leave. She took small, choppy breaths as regret almost suffocated her. Now she was trapped and she didn't know when she would get another chance to leave.

"Are we returning to Jazaar?" she asked huskily, her throat tight as panic pounded through her.

"Not yet," he said as he watched her carefully. "We're going to America."

Zoe gasped and she raised her hands to her mouth. *America.* Unshed tears burned her eyes and her heart swelled in her chest. After all these years she was returning home.

"Are you all right?" He grasped her elbow.

"Yes." She lowered her hands and noticed they were shaky. "I...I thought we weren't going to America because you didn't have any business there at the moment."

"I have to attend a few meetings," he said as he slowly released her arm. "I thought you'd be pleased. You keep suggesting a quick trip to the United States."

Alarm shot through her. Had she been that obvious?

She cast a quick glance at Nadir. He was alert. Watchful. Suspicion lurked in his dark eyes.

"Thank you," she said with a gracious smile as her heart thumped wildly. She stood on her tiptoes and grazed her lips against his cheek. "It's a wonderful surprise."

"Apparently."

She blushed at his dry tone. She wished she had controlled her response. She needed to be more careful. No way would she mess up right before she reached her goal. "What part of America?"

"New York City," he replied, his eyes never leaving her face. "We'll stay for a couple of days."

"I can't wait," she said, and she tenaciously held on to her gracious smile while she thought her heart was going to burst with relief. "I'll get dressed right away."

She hurried inside before Nadir could say a word or change his mind. A wild energy pulsed in her veins. She was going to be in America in a few hours. After all these years of wishing, dreaming and planning, it felt as if her mind was caught in a chaotic whirlwind.

Zoe looked over her shoulder and saw Nadir. His head was bent down as he punched something into his phone. She was ready to leave Jazaar, to abandon her old life. But was she prepared to abandon everything she had with him?

She didn't know. All these years she had thought she could walk away without a backward glance, but that was before she'd fallen in love with her husband.

He was a fool. Nadir gritted his teeth as he punched out a number on his phone. He'd seen the truth on her face. She wasn't able to hide it. Why hadn't he seen it sooner? Now he knew the real reason Zoe wanted so desperately to go to America.

He rubbed his forehead with tense fingers as he placed

the phone to his ear. He'd known something was up when Zoe, oh, so casually, kept suggesting a quick trip to the United States. It was more than a passing curiosity about the country where she had once lived. She was determined—no, *driven* to get to America.

But he had not quite figured out what she wanted in America. It turned out that she had given him all the evidence throughout their honeymoon. He had been too infatuated, too enamored with her, to put the clues together.

"Grayson?" he said when his head of security picked up the line. "I need you to track down someone in the United States and keep surveillance on him. His name? Musad Ali. He lives in Chicago."

Nadir disconnected the call and stared unseeingly into the blue water of the pool. He was tempted to cancel the trip to New York, but she would yearn for it even more. He'd take her and show her that there was nothing and no one waiting for her in America.

Once and for all, he would prove that all Zoe needed was him.

CHAPTER THIRTEEN

TIMES SQUARE was exactly what she'd expected. It was late at night, but the streets were bright and shining from all the lights. Zoe glanced at the large-screen television billboards that were several stories high. Lights of every color flashed before her eyes. Crowds of people choked the sidewalk. Vivid yellow New York cabs fought for an inch on Broadway. The scent of street vendors' salty pretzels wafted in the air.

The city was energizing. Loud. Big, bold and very American. And yet for some reason she didn't feel at home. She missed the peace and tranquility of the Jazaari desert.

It's only because you're not used to it, Zoe told herself as she and Nadir left the opulent theater where they had attended the opening night for a Broadway play. She had grown up in a quiet Houston suburb and spent the past several years in a much smaller village. She was simply out of practice. She would adapt quickly.

A limousine was waiting for them at the exit. Zoe paused and looked at Nadir. He was stunning in his black tuxedo and wore it with enviable ease. The suit emphasized his athletic physique and hinted at his glamorous life.

"Let's walk back to the hotel," she suggested. "It's not that far away."

Nadir gave her an indulgent look. "You can't get enough of this city."

She smiled in response as he dismissed the limo driver. She liked New York City, but she wouldn't have enjoyed it without him. Nadir was the perfect guide. He was entertaining, attentive and fascinating. When she was with him her day was full and exciting. It was going to be difficult giving all this up for a life of narrow focus and solitude.

Nadir rested his hand on her back as he guided her along the sidewalk. The front of the theater was packed with women dripping in diamonds and men in white scarves and black ties. None of the men could compare to the elegance and masculine beauty of her husband.

She walked through the crowd, inhaling the mingled perfumes and brushing up against fur coats and sequined jackets. Celebrities, politicians and titans of industry hustled to get a chance to speak to Nadir. It suddenly dawned on Zoe that this would be the perfect time to disappear. She slowed her step as she considered the opportunity.

It was nighttime and there was a big crowd. Most of the people were focused on Nadir. She started to breathe faster, her hands growing cold as she contemplated her next move. She was in the middle of a jostling crowd and that was a security team's nightmare. She knew from sight-seeing earlier that a subway station was nearby. What was stopping her?

But as the thought crossed her mind she rejected the idea. She wasn't prepared. The blood kept pumping hard through her veins as she looked around, noticing all the escape options. She couldn't do it. She couldn't walk away from Nadir like this.

She knew he would be sick with worry. He would tear this city apart looking for her, believing she was lost or in danger in this overwhelming place. His protective streak was often an obstacle, but it felt good to have someone strong and powerful looking out for her best interests.

Zoe reached out at her side and immediately found Nadir's hand. He slid his large, warm palm against hers before lacing their fingers together. With a simple touch Zoe felt safe and cared for. She didn't have to look for him to know he was there, ready to take her hand.

Would she ever be ready to leave him?

Zoe bit her lip as the thought flickered in her mind. She had no answer, and that worried her. Sensing Nadir's gaze on her, she glanced up and found him watching her. His harsh features were softened, his dark eyes gleaming, and there was a hint of a smile on his hard mouth.

"Thank you for taking me to the play," she said.

"It was my pleasure." His voice was a sexy rumble.

A slow heat suffused her body. She was acutely aware of how her red evening gown hugged her curves and the way her soft wrap brushed her skin. The past week had been all about pleasure.

"What did you think of it?" she asked.

"I enjoyed watching you the most." He leaned forward and whispered in her ear. "I find your enthusiasm very sexy. And you find everything in this city exciting."

"You can't blame me," she said with a laugh. Everything she did with Nadir was brighter and sweeter. Better. There was only one explanation for it. "I'm still on my honeymoon."

They had spent most of their time exploring Manhattan, walking hand-in-hand through Central Park and strolling through shops and museums. Leisurely lunches had a tendency to last for hours as they talked and laughed. Their evenings had been filled with the theater, sporting events and the most exclusive lounges.

And the nights they shared were magical. Nadir made

love to her with an intensity that blew away all her inhibitions. She couldn't deny him anything.

She wondered if their married life would continue this way, or if the connection she felt with him was just a little honeymoon enchantment. Would Nadir continue to make their time together a priority? Right now he didn't want any interruptions or distractions, but how long would that last? This week Nadir had gone so far as to turn off his phone when they were together. That simple gesture was more important to her than their trip to a famous jewelry store after-hours.

"Are you sure you're able to take all this time off from work?" she asked as they waited at a crosswalk for the light to change. "I don't want to wake up in the middle of the night and find you working."

Nadir gave a slanted smile. "Why would I spend the night with my laptop when I have you in my bed?"

"Why indeed?" she replied as a blush warmed her face. She shyly ducked her head as they crossed the street. It was only when they were in bed that she could express her love and trust in Nadir.

Each day she fell a little more in love with him, but she wasn't confident about expressing it. They had an arranged marriage, after all. Emotions and love weren't part of the deal.

That was the real reason why she hadn't disappeared from his life the moment they arrived at the JFK airport. Zoe's mind clung to that thought as they passed by a ruby-red glass staircase. It wasn't because there had been no right time to escape, or because she was afraid of the unknown. It was because her love for Nadir was growing so strong that she was willing to risk her freedom to stay with him.

She shivered as the truth hit her. He pulled his hand

away from hers, only to wrap his arm around her shoulders. She sighed when he drew her close to him, inhaling the crisp autumn night and the faint sandalwood of his cologne.

"Cold?" Nadir murmured as they walked in tandem, hip to hip. "We're almost at the hotel."

Zoe leaned her head against his broad shoulder. What if she stayed with him? Would that be so bad? Her chest tightened as the forbidden thought floated through her mind. She had never allowed herself to think of the possibility, yet it had drifted around her like a shadow for the past week.

As they entered the stunning lobby of the luxury hotel Zoe allowed herself to consider the question. Nadir wasn't like the men she knew. She could get an education and she could travel with him. She wouldn't live with the relatives who were the main source of her misery in Jazaar.

But she couldn't give up her dreams of practicing medicine now. Not after such a long struggle. Not when she had finally set foot on American soil.

If she went back to Jazaar with Nadir she'd have to give up the future she'd planned. She wouldn't get the chance to fulfill her dream of becoming a doctor.

Was she willing to throw away what she had for something that might come true? What she had with Nadir would develop into something strong and everlasting. She would never meet another man like him, and could never love anyone as she loved him.

And what were her chances of becoming a doctor? Zoe frowned as she entered the private elevator with her husband. She hated to ponder the possibility of failure. There were many people who pursued a medical career and didn't make it. What made her any different? She didn't even know if she could get into a university.

Nadir, on the other hand, had offered her a great opportunity to work with the health ministry. She knew that if she worked hard she could make a difference. It wasn't her dream, but it was something. It was close enough.

He was also offering her something she had always thought out of reach: a family. There was no family waiting for her in Houston, and she had always known that she would be alone there, trying to survive and follow her dream. After living with her relatives, after her relationship with Musad, she had thought she wanted to be alone.

As the elevator doors closed she stared blindly at the floor numbers flashing on the screen. Was she really considering changing her goals this late in the game? Could she stay with a man known as The Beast?

"You've grown very quiet," Nadir said as he raised her hand to his mouth and brushed his lips against her fingertips. "What are you thinking about?"

His question snapped her out of her reverie. "Actually, I was wondering about your nickname."

Nadir went very still. "What about it?"

"What really happened on your wedding night with Yusra?" Zoe wasn't sure if she was ready for the answer. She might have built an image of Nadir up in her mind. Maybe he *was* The Beast and she refused to see it.

Nadir pushed a button to pause the elevator. "Why do you want to know?"

She shrugged. "It doesn't make sense to me. You use the reputation to intimidate your opponents, but I know you're not a violent man."

Nadir looked steadily into her eyes. He showed no expression, but she sensed he was on guard. "Yusra miscarried after the ceremony."

"Oh." Her chest tightened. He'd had a relationship with Yusra. Of course he had. Yusra was gorgeous and the perfect Jazaari woman. Jealousy twisted inside her. Not only had they had a love-match, but Yusra had been carrying his child. "I thought you'd had an arranged marriage."

"It *was* an arranged marriage," he explained slowly. "The baby wasn't mine."

Zoe's mouth dropped open. "No way. Yusra? I can't wrap my mind around that. Who was the father?"

"I don't know. She wasn't going to confide in me."

"All that blood and the pain. A miscarriage would explain it. I'm surprised no one considered that possibility. They were far too willing to believe Yusra's side of the story."

"I should have handled the situation better," Nadir admitted as he looked away. "I could have annulled the wedding in a less spectacular fashion. I was angry, and during that time I allowed my emotions to rule my head."

"But you had to sever the relationship?" She knew Nadir could never stay with a woman who betrayed him. "You couldn't trust her after that?"

He nodded slowly. "I never told anyone outside my family."

And now he was sharing the secret with her. Zoe understood the significance in that and wasn't going to take it lightly. She squeezed his hand. "You should have defended yourself when the gossip started."

"No, that would have placed Yusra in a dangerous position. I was furious with her, but she would have been punished for sex outside of marriage. It was difficult enough to keep her hospital information a secret."

"I should have known that was what happened." She had instinctively known that Nadir hadn't hurt his first wife, but she could have put the medical clues together.

"How would you?"

"Give me some credit. I've been your wife for over a

month. I've seen you at your best and at your worst. I know you could never hurt a woman."

Nadir rested his forehead on hers and sighed. "Thank you, Zoe."

"But you didn't need to adopt The Beast reputation," she said softly. "I'm sure there are some people who would have believed in you."

"You believe in me." He brushed his lips against hers. "That's all I need."

And she had believed in him for a while. Zoe wasn't sure when she'd started to see past his reputation. She wouldn't have lain in bed with Nadir if she'd suspected he was abusive. She wouldn't have considered staying married to him if she'd thought he had the potential to be violent.

And she *was* going to stay with him, she decided as the nervousness bubbled up inside her. She could be married to a man known as The Beast because she knew the truth.

She needed to be with him. They were a team. A couple. She easily imagined building a future together and eventually creating a family. She wanted this dream even if it meant giving up the idea of becoming a doctor.

"No more talk about Yusra," Nadir said. "Instead, I want to take you dancing. We can go to the nightclub you mentioned."

"It will only take me a few minutes to change." Zoe leaned into him, absorbing his heat and strength. "And what shall we do tomorrow?"

"Whatever you want," he promised as he slid his hand along the length of her arm. "Tomorrow is our last day here."

The idea suddenly made her jumpy. Her pulse began to accelerate and she pulled away from him. "And then we return to Jazaar?" She'd meant to sound casual, but her voice came out high and reedy.

"Yes."

She felt a bead of sweat on her forehead and her stomach cramped with anxiety. She felt trapped, caged in the elevator. What was wrong with her? She had made up her mind, but her instincts hadn't gotten the message.

Was it a good idea to return to the place she had tried so hard to escape? She brushed her forehead with a shaky hand. Was she thinking this through enough?

Nadir turned and cradled her face in his hand. When he caressed her mouth with a kiss she closed her eyes and melted into him. The panic blurred and the anxious questions faded away as she returned the kiss.

Yes, she was making the right decision. She was going to survive in Jazaar. This time she had Nadir at her side. This time she would thrive.

She barely heard the chime and reluctantly broke the kiss the moment the private elevator opened into the penthouse suite. She saw the sensual promise in his eyes and felt the curl of excitement low in her belly.

As they crossed the threshold to the entry room, she saw the butler approach.

"Good evening, Your Highnesses," the tall young man said. "I trust you enjoyed the play?"

"Yes, we did," Zoe answered with a bright smile as Nadir helped remove her wrap. "Thank you."

"You have a visitor," the butler informed Nadir as he accepted their coats.

Zoe saw a movement in the corner of her eye. She turned to see Nadir's brother Rashid step out of the balcony that overlooked Times Square and into the room. While he wore a T-shirt, jeans and sneakers, his mood was anything but casual. He appeared just as unfriendly as when she'd met him briefly at her wedding ceremony.

As she greeted him with a polite smile, she saw a disapproving look in his eyes before he ignored her completely. Zoe wasn't sure why, but she sensed that her honeymoon was officially over.

"Rashid, your manners need to improve," Nadir said as he watched Zoe enter the bedroom to change for the night-club. He waited until she'd closed the door before he turned his attention on his brother. "Not only have you crashed my honeymoon, but you were bordering on rude to Zoe."

Rashid shrugged off the reprimand. Nadir frowned at his brother's attitude. His brother should make an attempt to welcome his bride into the family. What did he have against Zoe?

"There'd better be a good reason why you're here," he said as he invited Rashid to sit down. Under normal circumstances he would be happy to see his brother, but he didn't want the world to intrude on his relationship with his wife. He wanted to focus on his marriage and build a solid foundation.

"Your honeymoon has lasted for over a month." Rashid leaned back and spread his arms on the back of the sofa.

"I have also conducted business." Nadir silently admitted to himself that he hadn't kept to his usual brutal schedule. He did his duty, but Zoe was his priority.

"I'm just relaying a message from our father." Rashid hooked one foot over his knee. "You are a sheikh and you are needed to deal with matters of the state."

"And I will return the day after tomorrow." Nadir strolled over to the window and looked out at the iconic view. "Couldn't this have waited?"

"I wanted to give you an idea of what you are facing." Rashid rose from his seat and walked over to stand next to his brother. "Many people have declared that The Beast has been tamed by his American bride."

Tamed? Nadir scoffed at the suggestion. When it came to Zoe, he didn't feel very civilized. Just the thought of her made him passionate and territorial. "Soon they will forget that nickname."

"Because they think you've become soft," Rashid argued. "Many of your progressive ideas are now under attack because you aren't perceived as ruthless anymore."

"Ridiculous. I will show them not to underestimate me." And once his country got to know Zoe they would admire and love her as their future Sultana. "That reminds me I want to add Zoe to the health ministry. She is very interested in medicine and she has worked in women's health for years."

Rashid reared back. His mouth sagged open as he stared at Nadir. "You can't be serious," he whispered in horror.

"Why would you say that?"

"You married for political reasons." Rashid swept his arm out and pointed at the bedroom door. "Zoe Martin is a means to an end."

Nadir's jaw tightened as he controlled his temper. He didn't like Rashid's tone. His brother would soon learn that what had started out as an arranged marriage was proving to be his most important relationship.

"And now you've taken her on a lavish trip." He gestured at the penthouse suite. "Rumor has it that you take her advice. That you seek her counsel. And now all of sudden she's getting a powerful position in the kingdom? She must be very good in bed."

Nadir grabbed his brother by the shirt and pinned him against the window. "Be very careful how you speak about Zoe," he said in a low growl. "She is my wife."

"She is your blind spot," Rashid countered. "Marrying her was supposed to solve your problem with that tribe. Instead she has Westernized you."

"You think someone could dictate how I act?"

"I didn't think so until you met Zoe." Rashid pulled his shirt from Nadir's grasp. "But talk in the business world says otherwise. They say you are so besotted with her that you can't think straight."

Nadir arched an eyebrow. "The businessmen in Athens may not agree with you." Mexico City was another matter, but after discussing his strategy with Zoe he had miraculously triumphed.

"You're not as focused," Rashid insisted. "Not as driven. Your wife is becoming a dangerous distraction."

"So what if I'm not at every meeting or if I can't be reached every second of the day?" Nadir asked, his irritation sharpening his tone. "I don't have to explain my actions."

"I think you're acting like a fool with your wife. Giving her a place on the health ministry?" Rashid groaned at the thought. "What is *wrong* with you?"

He was falling for Zoe. Hard. That didn't mean that his decision-making was faulty. If anything, his eyes had been opened. Zoe was the wife he needed when he became Sultan.

"What happened to your plans?" his brother complained. "You were going to send her to the palace in the mountains. She was going to stay there out of the way so you could get back to your life in Omaira."

"So?" He had made those plans when he didn't know Zoe. Now he knew he couldn't live without her.

"Zoe is a liability. You need to stop stalling and follow your plan. The sooner the better."

Zoe slowly closed the bedroom door and staggered back. Her heart was racing, her stomach curling. She felt sick as Rashid's words spun in her head.

Nadir was going to pack her off to the mountains. The room whirled and slanted and she grabbed onto the back of a chair. He wanted to send her somewhere isolated and forget her while he returned to his life. It would be business as usual for him, purgatory for her.

The stinging news cut through her. Zoe's knees slowly buckled and she clumsily sat down. She couldn't believe it. She slowly shook her head as she stared at the closed door. Nadir had played her well.

She didn't trust anyone but she had believed in him. She had thought he cared for her, maybe even felt something like affection. But she had been mistaken. Nadir was only enjoying the sexual chemistry they shared.

She placed her head in her hands and drew in shallow breaths as she fought back nausea. She felt as if she had just dodged a bullet. She had almost given up her dream for Nadir. For a *man,* she thought bitterly.

It was sickening. Horrifying. She had been so close to her goal and had almost turned her back on it for the promise of something stronger. Deeper. Imaginary.

Zoe winced at her stupidity. Had the ministry offer been a lie? Had the caresses and late-night talks been pretend? She wanted to believe that Nadir had meant all that, but now she wasn't sure.

Her arms and legs started to shake. She wanted to run. Hide. Weep. She couldn't…not yet. Not until she had disappeared for good.

She had to behave as if her world hadn't turned upside down. That meant she couldn't hide in her room and lick her wounds. Zoe slowly rose from her chair on unsteady feet.

Now she needed to act as if she was a happy bride on her honeymoon. It hurt to think of the way she'd felt just a few minutes ago. How blissful, how incredibly ignorant she had been of Nadir's plans.

She blinked back tears and took a deep breath. She had to try. If she could successfully pretend to be a shy, virginal bride on her wedding night, then she could do this. Nadir expected to see a wildly naïve woman, Zoe decided with a spurt of anger. She wouldn't have to put up the act for long before she disappeared into the night.

She straightened her shoulders and flipped back her hair. The anger inside her started to grow, flaring hot and bitter, eating away at her. She took a deep breath and pasted on a smile. It was showtime.

She swung the door open and strode into the sitting room. She looked in the direction of the men, careful not to make eye contact with Nadir as they turned to her. She sashayed her hips as if she was ready to party.

"I'm sorry I took so long," she said to Nadir without looking in his direction. "Rashid, are you going night-clubbing with us?"

Rashid chose not to answer. Somehow she had expected that. What was the point of communicating with a sister-in-law when she was going to be thrown into a prison for the rest of her life?

"Nightclubbing?" Nadir stared at her light blue bandage dress and skyscraper heels.

She saw the sexual heat in his eyes. Her traitorous body responded eagerly, her nipples rasping against her bra. Zoe was tempted to tease him before declaring he could never touch her again. *Never again.*

"I'm sorry, Zoe," Nadir said with what sounded like true regret. "We won't be able to go tonight. Something came up."

"Oh, that's a shame." She gave a pout and saw Nadir's

gaze settle on her lips. She'd rather he watch her mouth than read her eyes. "Well, I can go by myself."

"Go…by yourself?" Nadir repeated dully as Rashid's jaw dropped.

"I'll be all right." She brushed off his concern with an ebullient wave of her hand. Wild emotions churned inside her as she hurried for the elevator. The click of her heels echoed the fast beat of her heart. "I have a security team. Nothing will happen to me."

"You are *not* going to a club."

Nadir's harsh tone would make anyone obey, but Zoe was beyond listening. She needed to escape before they returned to Jazaar. She needed to get away from Nadir before she talked herself into staying with him.

"But you'll be busy." She didn't look back and pressed the elevator button. *Open… Open… Please open…*

"Zoe, you will stay here." He was at her side just as the elevator doors opened. He cupped her elbow and turned her to face him. "In fact, the urgent work I have won't take too long. Rashid and I will work here."

Damn, she had played it all wrong. Despair clawed at her chest. She had to get out of here, had to disappear, but Nadir wasn't letting her out of his sight. So much for slipping out of his life while he wasn't looking.

"Download an e-book," he suggested as he guided her away from the elevator. "I'll be in soon."

"If you insist." She wasn't going to get out tonight. She'd have to bide her time. "Goodnight, Rashid," she said with a smile.

Rashid didn't say a word and turned away. Yeah, that guy didn't like her at all, Zoe decided as she kept her smile steady.

"Goodnight, Nadir." She brushed her lips against his

cheek and stepped back before he could deepen the kiss. She hurried to the bedroom as tears threatened to fall.

She should have known better. The scent, the feel, the heat of him had brought on a cascade of emotions. She never should have gotten close to him. She should have left when she had a chance. But she was going to make up for the mistake now.

CHAPTER FOURTEEN

"GONE?" Nadir's head snapped up as panic blazed through his veins. He stared at Grayson, his head of security, standing in the center of his office. "What do you mean that Zoe is gone? Gone where?"

Nadir remained very still as dark emotions burned through him like acid. He restrained himself from jumping into action. He wanted to go out into the city and tear it apart. He needed to find her and bring her back safe.

"We don't know, Your Highness," Grayson admitted.

The man showed no expression, but Nadir could tell that he was shaken by the security breach.

"We lost her around the Rockefeller Plaza."

Zoe was gone.

The words rippled in head. He had spent all night going over business with Rashid. When he'd looked in on her this morning Zoe had still been fast asleep. He had been tempted to wake her up, but he'd had a breakfast meeting he couldn't afford to miss.

He rubbed his hand over his face. *Gone.* He should have kept a closer eye, but he had grown too arrogant. Too complacent.

"The best-case scenario is that Zoe has got lost, but it's unlikely. We would have spotted her."

"She's been gone for an hour?" Nadir dropped his hands

and sprang from his chair. He began to pace behind his desk. He should have been contacted immediately. "Zoe's not lost. She would have returned to the hotel."

"We have all systems in place," Grayson assured him. "If it's a kidnapping the phones are—"

"It's not a kidnapping," Nadir said, and stopped in front of the window that overlooked the Hudson River. Zoe had wanted to come to America from the moment they were married. There was only one thing that had driven her here. Nadir's eyes narrowed into slits as jealousy roared to life. One person.

"We contacted the butler at your hotel suite," Grayson informed him. "The Sheikha didn't pack a bag. Nothing is missing."

Nadir's mouth twisted. Even his security detail had considered the possibility that Zoe had left him. He had not seen it coming. He had done everything to make her happy and satisfied. Where had he failed?

"Check on the whereabouts of Musad Ali," Nadir said in a low growl. He glanced up at the gray skies. "If you find him, you'll find Zoe."

He had to admit the truth: Musad was the real reason why Zoe had married The Beast. It hadn't just been to get out of her uncle's house or out of Jazaar. She wanted to be with her lover.

Nadir closed his eyes as he fought off a wave of dizziness. The blood roared in his ears. He slowly opened his eyes. He wasn't going to let her go without a fight.

Zoe was his wife. Every action he made was to protect and care for his woman. Their relationship would always be his top priority. He had thought this honeymoon would demonstrate his commitment to her.

"She can't have gotten far," Grayson said, his voice

sounding far away, although he hadn't moved. "I'll check the airlines, car rentals, bus and train depots."

Zoe had been acting differently since they came to America. She'd been quieter and often lost in thought. Many times he had caught her staring out the window or staring at her hands. Had she spent those moments day-dreaming about her lover and planning her rendezvous?

"It's a damn shame she doesn't have a cell phone," Grayson muttered. "We could have tracked her GPS."

Nadir froze as a glimmer of hope flickered inside him. He slowly lifted his head and turned to Grayson. "There *is* a way we can track her."

"Good. How do you want me to retrieve her?"

Nadir slowly exhaled. "We don't." He barely got the words out. "We let her go."

A few months later

"Are you sure you want to go home, Zoe?" Cathy asked as they stood in front of Zoe's apartment building. "It's not even midnight."

"Thanks, but tomorrow is my first day of work," Zoe said to the small group of friends. "I can't waltz in there after partying all night."

"All right, all right," Cathy conceded. "We understand."

"Goodnight!" Zoe said with a wave. She enjoyed hanging out with the group of college students. They didn't have a lot in common, but she wasn't so lonely when she was with them.

She had been in Houston, Texas, for only a few months, and thanks to a few pawn shops and the haggling talent she'd picked up in Jazaar she had managed to finance a few things on her dream list. She had passed her high school equivalency test and would soon go to night classes at the community college. Tomorrow she would be a receptionist at a doctor's office. It was nowhere close to her dream of becoming a doctor, but it was a step in the right direction.

Returning to Houston hadn't been the homecoming she had envisioned during her dark, lonely days in Jazaar. Once she had gained her freedom Zoe had been compelled to return to her hometown. She had thought she would feel peace or relief once she stepped onto Texas soil. Instead she had felt lost and disoriented.

Her childhood home had been torn down for new housing. Friends had moved away. The hospital that had been a second home to her had changed so much that it was barely recognizable. There was very little to remind her of her parents. She only had their graves to visit.

When she stood at the cemetery and stared at their simple gravestones Zoe knew she had to push on and continue her family's work. She had no pictures or heirlooms to keep the memories alive, but she had always felt close to her parents when she practiced medicine.

Zoe was slowly rebuilding her life and had even got a place of her own. She glanced up at the large, nondescript building. The small studio apartment barely fit a table and a sofabed. That was all she needed for now, and it was all hers.

As she opened the security door she realized her friend Timothy was at her side.

"I'll walk you up," he offered, and held the door for her.

"That's very sweet of you, but I can manage." All her new friends were protective of her. They could tell she wasn't familiar with city life.

"I insist." He grasped her elbow and led her into the building.

Zoe held her tongue as they walked through the corridor. Timothy would find out soon enough that she could take care of herself. He didn't know much about her life. None of her new friends did. She was still a little reserved with them and hadn't shared much of her past. They probably wouldn't believe her. What sheikha wore clothes from a charity thrift shop?

If she *was* still a sheikha… She had had no contact with her husband. Nadir had never found her. Had he even looked for her? Or was he looking for another wife? Someone more suitable?

She pushed the thought away when she reached her door, Zoe grabbed her keys. "I should be fine, now," Zoe said. "Thanks, Timothy."

"No problem." He rested his arm against the doorframe and leaned in. "Good luck on your first day of work."

"Thanks. I'm a little nervous," she admitted. She had worked so hard to get to this point. What if it wasn't worth it?

"You'll do great," he said, before placing his hand on her shoulder. "We should celebrate tomorrow night."

"I would love to, but most of the gang has class tomorrow."

"I meant just the two of us." He squeezed her shoulder. "Like a date."

She dropped her keys. Zoe bent down quickly to retrieve them as her mind whirled. She'd had no idea Timothy was interested in her.

She wished she was interested in him. He was a nice guy. He was supportive, kind and hard-working. He was also handsome and fun to be around. He was safe.

But he was no Nadir.

And that was the problem. Zoe closed her eyes shut as grief and regret slammed through her. She was still in love with her husband. Missed him so much that it hurt. She couldn't imagine being with another man.

"Thanks, Timothy, but I can't," she replied as she rose to her full height, clenching the keys in her hand. "I just got out of a relationship and…"

He held up his hands in surrender. "Say no more. I understand. The time isn't right."

"Exactly." She was grateful that she didn't have to deal with any drama. That was another thing she liked about Timothy. There were no highs or lows. Life was calm around him.

"So I'll wait."

Zoe gritted her teeth. Waiting wasn't going to change anything. She could never feel for Timothy what she felt for Nadir. There was no spark, no passion. She couldn't imagine sacrificing all her dreams for Timothy.

And that was probably a good thing.

"I'll text you tomorrow to see how the job went," Timothy promised. He kissed her cheek, letting his lips linger on her cool skin. "Sweet dreams."

"Goodnight," she replied softly, and watched him leave. She wasn't sure what had brought that on. She had never shown any romantic interest in him. Or in any man for that matter. She had had tunnel vision from the moment she'd disappeared in Rockefeller Plaza.

She shook her head and entered her apartment. She flipped on the lights and gasped. Her heart lurched when saw Nadir sitting on her sofabed. Hot, swirling energy roared between them.

He had come to reclaim his bride.

"Nadir!" She stared into his eyes, unable to look away, to move. He looked menacing in a black designer suit. He sat quietly, but there was nothing casual about him. He was alert. Watchful. Ready to pounce.

"Who's loverboy?" he asked in a low growl.

"What are you doing here?" All of her nerve-endings

had sparked to life. Emotions swirled inside her, threatening to burst. One moment she felt comatose, and now she felt violently alive. "How did you get in?"

"I've come to take you home."

Home? No—more like prison. He wanted to send her to the remote regions of Jazaar. She knew she should dash outside and get away as fast as she could. But it would be of no use. Nadir wouldn't lose her twice.

"How did you find me?" Her voice croaked.

Nadir slowly stood. "Your e-book reader has Wi-Fi. My security team was able to triangulate your coordinates the first day you disappeared."

A humorless smile tugged at the corner of her mouth. She had left all of Nadir's gifts behind but she had forgotten that the e-reader was in her purse. She had eventually hocked it, along with everything else she had. It had hurt giving up that one gift.

"You've always known where I've been?" Her eyes narrowed with suspicion. "I don't believe you."

"I let you go because I thought I finally knew the real reason you married The Beast," Nadir said softly, almost nonchalantly. "Getting out of your uncle's house was only the first phase in your plans."

She didn't say anything. There was no point; it was true. Nadir had figured it all out.

"But you couldn't leave Jazaar unless you were accompanied by a male relative," he continued as he took a step closer. "Your Uncle Tareef wanted to keep you under lock and key. You didn't have anyone in your family who would cross your uncle. Fortunately, a husband would do."

Zoe gritted her teeth. She would not feel guilty. She would *not*. Nadir had had his reasons for marrying her. It pushed along his goals. She had the same right to go after her dreams.

"I thought you wanted to go to America for sentimental reasons." A muscle bunched in his jaw. "It was only while we were in Mexico City that I suspected the truth."

Of course. That was when she had attended the medical conference. Nadir had realized she wouldn't give up her dreams. "And yet we still traveled to America?"

Nadir shrugged his shoulder but she saw a glimpse of stark pain in his eyes. "I guess I was arrogant enough to believe that you would choose me."

She *had* chosen him—up to the moment when she'd heard of his plans. But she did not want to let him know she had been so weak. Zoe pressed her lips together. She wouldn't give him the satisfaction.

Nadir gave a deep sigh. "But my sacrifice was for nothing. You didn't meet with him. You didn't make any contact, didn't even try."

Zoe frowned. "Meet with whom?"

"Musad Ali," he said in an angry hiss. "Your first love."

Zoe stared at him and comprehension slowly dawned on her. "You think I did all this to get out of the country so I could rendezvous with…Musad?"

He nodded sharply.

"This is unbelievable. You think I went through all this to reunite with a man who treated me like dirt?" Zoe placed her hands on her hips. "What kind of woman do you think I am? Do you really believe that I would want to be with someone who abandoned me and exposed me to dangerous gossip?"

"What was I supposed to think?"

She glared at Nadir. "The only reason I would hunt Musad down is to kick his ass. But, honestly, he isn't worth the effort."

"You say that now because he stood you up."

"Let me make it clear," she said as anger flushed her

cheeks. "Musad is my ex-lover. Emphasis on *ex*. I am not in love with him and I was never in love with him."

"Then why did you escape from your security detail that day?" Nadir asked. "Why did you leave me?"

"Because I was ready to sacrifice every dream I had to be with you." She had been too caught up in the make-believe. It had felt real. Strong. Lasting. But it had been just a fantasy that had almost cost her her dreams. Her freedom. "I didn't know about your plans," she accused. "You had no intention of having a relationship with me once the honeymoon was over."

Nadir took a step back. "I never said that."

Zoe's mouth twisted with disgust. He was still lying to her. "I heard you, Nadir. I heard you talking to Rashid on our last night together. You planned on dumping me in the mountains of Jazaar."

Nadir muttered a savage oath and speared his fingers into his hair. "That was before I met you."

"You mean that was before you discovered there was sexual chemistry between us." Zoe crossed her arms. "That's why you allowed me to go on your business trip. Otherwise I would be trapped."

Nadir clenched his jaw. "I'd like to think that what we have is more than sexual chemistry."

"It *was*. It was a lot more for me," she confessed, and she felt tears threatening to spill over her lashes. "I learned how to trust you even when I was risking everything to be at your side. I was ready to give up my dreams for you. I was prepared to follow you back to Jazaar because I love you."

Shock chased across his face. Hadn't he known how she felt? How could he not have known? Wasn't it obvious in the way she lit up when he entered a room or in the way she kissed him? She had placed her trust in him again and again. She didn't do that for just anyone.

"I actually thought I could return to Jazaar, the one place I swore I would never visit again." She felt a teardrop trail down her cheek and angrily brushed it away. "I knew that you didn't love me back, but when I was with you I felt loved and cared for. And it all turned out to be a lie."

"It's not a lie." Nadir reached for her, but she backed away, her spine hitting the door. "I love you, Zoe. I want you to come back."

Her breath hitched in her throat. He loved her? No, she wouldn't believe it. He was up to something. "I'm never coming back. Do you really think I can trust you after I found out about your plans?"

"I want to be with you. Every day. Every night." He took another step closer. "I want you at my side."

She shook her head. "Why? Why now after all these months?"

"I thought I was doing what was best for you. Letting you go was the hardest thing I've ever done," he confessed.

"But you didn't let go. Not really. You were tracking me all this time."

"I had to make sure you were safe. I stayed away so you could live the way you wanted. But I can't let you go," he said rawly. "I need you in my life."

"No, you don't. You need to find another wife. I'm the worst sheikha in history. I'm not a proper Jazaari woman." Her voice rose as he kept advancing. "I'm a liability."

"That's not true." He placed his hands against the door, effectively caging her. He surrounded her but was careful not to touch. As if he didn't trust his restraint. "You are the wife I want. You are the advisor I need. We make a great team."

"No." She didn't want to remember those times. The

moments when she had felt connected with Nadir. When she had believed they belonged together.

"Zoe," he said in a low, pleading tone. He rested his forehead against hers. "I make sacrifices every day to perform my duty. I've given up a lot to fulfill my destiny. But I won't give up *you*."

He brushed his lips against hers. The faint touch sent shockwaves through her body. It took all of Zoe's willpower to remain still.

"Please, Zoe," Nadir's voice cracked with emotion. "Please give our marriage a chance. I can't live without you."

"And I can't live *with* you," Zoe whispered. She flattened her hands against his chest and tried to push him away. "Not in Jazaar. Not in a royal life that keeps me from what I'm meant to do."

"I will do everything in my power to protect you and your dreams," he promised, clasping his hands around hers.

She noticed how his hands shook.

"You will have the best tutors so you can get your medical degree."

She froze. "The palace won't allow that."

"The two of us will fight for it. As a team. And we'll fight for your right to practice medicine."

"That's going to be a battle." An ugly, bitter fight that could weaken his position in the kingdom.

"It'll be worth the fight." He lifted her hand and pressed his mouth against her palm. "And you can travel whenever you want. Without a male relative's permission."

Hope flared inside her. "Wouldn't you worry that I would run away?"

"I trust you."

She looked in his eyes and knew he spoke the truth.

Even if she ran away, he trusted that she would return to him again and again.

Zoe wished she was brave. She wanted to go with him, but she was too afraid. "Nadir...I just don't know if I can return to Jazaar. I always felt trapped there."

"I know."

"I want to be with you," she admitted, "but I don't know if I can take that risk."

"Which is why we'll stay here."

Zoe's eyes widened. Had she heard him correctly? "Here? In Texas? But you have to be in Jazaar. You said so yourself."

"We will have a home here and one in Jazaar. I will make trips to my homeland when it's necessary. You can return to Jazaar when you're ready."

His homeland was important to him. She couldn't allow him to give that up. As cosmopolitan as Nadir was, he thrived in the desert. "But Jazaar..."

"Is going through many changes," Nadir insisted. "When I returned to Jazaar I saw the kingdom through your eyes. I've been making it a place where you can feel safe and free."

"You did all that? For me?" She cupped his face with her hands and stared at him in wonder. "But what if I'm never ready to return?"

"Then we will make our home elsewhere," he promised. "I will live where you want. Tell me you're willing to give us another chance."

She stared into his eyes, her heart pounding fiercely as she took the leap of faith. "Yes, Nadir. I want to share my life with you. I want another chance."

Triumph shone in his dark eyes. "You won't regret it, Zoe. I promise."

"I believe you," she said with a tremulous smile, before Nadir captured her mouth with his in a hard kiss.

EPILOGUE

Two years later

ZOE sat in front of Nadir on his powerful Arabian horse as they watched the sun dip behind the sand dunes of Jazaar. A cooling breeze tugged against her caftan, but she felt warm and secure in his arms. She smiled as the colors of saffron and gold streaked the sky.

"You're right," she said softly as she leaned her head against Nadir's shoulder. "A Jazaari sunset is one of the most beautiful sights of the world."

"I believe I said nothing can compare with it," Nadir murmured as he stroked her hair.

Zoe's skin tingled from his gentle touch. "I don't know if that's true. I haven't traveled as much as you. *Yet*," she clarified.

She had made several international trips alone in the past year to attend public health conferences. As much as she enjoyed the trips, and learned valuable information, she didn't like staying away from home for too long.

The gold streaks faded and the sky turned to sapphire. A sigh of satisfaction rumbled in Nadir's chest. "Jazaar is becoming more and more beautiful."

"I agree." He was the reason for that. He wasn't the Sultan, but through his power and connections her husband was slowly modernizing the kingdom. Zoe no longer saw Jazaar as a prison but rather as a burgeoning paradise. The desert was her home, her haven.

Nadir looked down at her. "You do?"

"Yes, I thought the dedication for the women's clinic today was a sight to behold." It had been a struggle getting the health ministry to listen to her, but she had made her voice heard.

"Your parents would have been honored at having the clinic named after them."

She nodded. "I can't wait to open more around the kingdom."

"And one day you'll work in those clinics."

Zoe heard the pride in his voice. "One day," she agreed. "It's probably a good thing I'm not going to any more conferences," she said as she patted her rounded stomach hidden under the folds of her caftan. "I'm staying close to home for the next year or two."

"Good idea." Nadir covered her hands with his. Zoe swallowed the lump in her throat at the sight of them cradling her pregnant belly. "Sure you won't get bored?"

She scoffed at the idea. "Are you kidding? My schedule is packed before this baby arrives."

She had so many dreams, and Nadir was making sure she had every opportunity to make them come true. Her life was so full that her world was only limited by her imagination.

"We should get back to the camp," Nadir said with a tinge of regret as he lightly tugged the horse's reins. "Your Arabic tutor will be waiting."

Okay, she loved *almost* every minute of her life. Reading and writing Arabic was more difficult than she had ever imagined. "Can I skip the lesson tonight?" she asked.

"Don't you want to read Jazaari folk tales to our baby?"

"At this rate our baby will have to read them to me."

He chuckled. "Perhaps you need another incentive. Wouldn't you like to read our marriage contract? Don't you want to know what I had to promise you?"

"No need." He supported her with her studies and encouraged her to make changes in the health ministry. He protected her and made sure she felt safe and loved. She had more than she had dared to dream. "You've given me everything I need."

Nadir curled his fingers under her chin and tilted her head so she could see his face. Her pulse quickened when she saw the love and devotion in his eyes.

"I love you, Zoe," he said as he reverently brushed his lips against hers.

Zoe reached up and cupped her hand against his cheek as she deepened the kiss. She knew he loved her, but she liked hearing it every day. Nadir wasn't going to let her down. He was the man she could trust and love. He was the man she could rely on.

"I love you, Nadir," Zoe said. "Let's go home."

* * * * *

& A sneaky peek at next month...

MODERN™

INTERNATIONAL AFFAIRS, SEDUCTION & PASSION GUARANTEED

My wish list for next month's titles...

In stores from 20th July 2012:

☐ Contract with Consequences – Miranda Lee

☐ The Man She Shouldn't Crave – Lucy Ellis

☐ A Tainted Beauty – Sharon Kendrick

☐ The Dangerous Jacob Wilde – Sandra Marton

In stores from 3rd August 2012:

☐ The Sheikh's Last Gamble – Trish Morey

☐ The Girl He'd Overlooked – Cathy Williams

☐ One Night With The Enemy – Abby Green

☐ His Last Chance at Redemption – Michelle Conder

☐ The Hidden Heart of Rico Rossi – Kate Hardy

Available at WHSmith, Tesco, Asda, Eason, Amazon and Apple

Just can't wait?

Visit us Online

You can buy our books online a month before they hit the shops! **www.millsandboon.co.uk**

0712/01

Special Offers

Every month we put together collections and longer reads written by your favourite authors.

Here are some of next month's highlights— and don't miss our fabulous discount online!

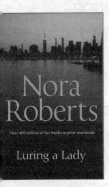

Nora Roberts

Over 400 million of her books in print worldwide

Luring a Lady

Hot nights with a SPANIARD

CAROLE MORTIMER   INDIA GREY   LYNN RAYE HARRIS

AT HIS SERVICE
HIS 9-5 SECRETARY

HELEN BROOKS   MICHELLE CELMER   JENNIE ADAMS

On sale 3rd August   On sale 3rd August   On sale 3rd August

Save 20%
on all Special Releases

Find out more at
www.millsandboon.co.uk/specialreleases

Visit us Online

0712/ST/MB381